O H I O

II

1 0

A. V. SMITH

Book Cover: Ray Southard, Seviinth Degree Productions, LLC

Editor: Tricia Barnes

Editor: Amy Vrana

Editing Consultant: Kristin Reeg

Warped Writing and Publishing, LLC, Columbus, Ohio

ISBN: 978-1735106939

DEDICATION

To my children, Devan, Naiya, and Christian:

My prayer to The Universe for you has been sent. You are

my life source; greatness awaits you.

I Love You.

TABLE OF CONTENTS

CHAPTER ONE
CRUSH GROOVE

Crush Groove

The restaurant nightclub on the first two levels had been completely packed with the grand opening going on. The loft area was separate, and from the insulation added between floors, the music was scarcely heard. Men with assault weapons strapped across their backs stood in the distance watching everything.

Security was a priority with so many executives of The

Organization in one place.

A thirty-foot oval bar was the center piece of the first room entered from the elevator, and the kitchen area still had cabinets left to be put in. The gray and white marble floor was a stunning contrast to the hanging lights and wall accessories, some areas of the floor still covered in plastic.

A seventeen by nine-foot Bubinga Slab Table with Raised Edges took up a large portion in the next area of the loft. From where it was situated, the balcony offered one of the best views of the city's skyline.

The people sitting at the table consisted of eight men and two women, each given responsibility to manage and control the money being made in their respective cities.

A large man walked in from an area off the main rooms. He wore a black tuxedo with a red handkerchief in his lapel. His presence was absolute.

"Ladies and gentlemen, pimps, and pushers, welcome to my newest endeavor. Forgive the mess, we had to concentrate on getting the money maker opened, and from the guest list tonight, we are making inroads across the Midwest. Soon we will be branching into the Southern States. I couldn't do it without you all." He walked to the table and lifted a bottle of very expensive whiskey given as a gift to him.

"Detroit Black has brought The Macallan Forty-Year-Old Single Malt Scotch Whiskey to help celebrate tonight and the box of Cohiba Behike from my friend in Cleveland will go nicely."

The man had an associate open the bottle of whiskey and place it back on the table before he passed out cigars to everyone.

"These are Crystal Whiskey Glasses I had made for special occasions like this. I hope my Crest on them will inspire you all to see the bigger picture." He paused as he retrieved the Macallan Whiskey.

"The briefcases by your seats are a token of my gratitude."

"Thanks Crush." The voices at the table spoke up in appreciation.

"It's important to know that I can trust you to do what I pay you to do without fail, and for the most part each one of you have succeeded." He finished pouring the whiskey into the glasses, leaving a minuscule amount in the bottle.

"Before we engage in celebration there's one bit of housekeeping we need to discuss."

Without warning Crusher took the bottle of whiskey and slammed it across the head of one of his guests. The sound dulled out every other noise in the 2300 square foot loft.

The person struck immediately fell from his chair.

Crusher hit him again and the blood splattered across the two people sitting closest to him.

The man fell from his chair onto the floor with his body convulsing in spasms, but Crusher kept slamming the bottle into his head.

"I hear everything before it's spoken. I know everything before it's thought. When you skim and sell on the side, its being disloyal. When you take product from us and sell it on the side, it's being disloyal." Crusher hit the man one last time and walked back to his seat with the bottle in hand.

"Spade, find his brother and family. Let me know when you do." He gave his bodyguard an order who then quickly disappeared into another portion of the loft.

"Now, to my family. I appreciate you, and I demand loyalty." They raised their glasses and lit cigars as the untrustworthy member labored for breath until he died.

The hours passed, and the guests filtered out back to their respective cities. Crusher had made his point. Loyalty was essential, and a lack of this same quality led to death. He stood on the balcony looking down at the line formed to enter his club.

"Sir, we've located them both." His personal bodyguard emerged from inside the loft. Crusher looked up toward the sky before walking to meet his bodyguard.

"I need to change." Whether in his tuxedo or jeans and black hoodie, Derrick Crusher had power.

"I want to deal with this personally. Is the car ready?"

Derrick walked back to the table to pour a shot of the Macallan Whiskey. The bottle, now cleaned as if brand new, was cemented into the minds of those who had witnessed the eruption earlier.

"I want Georgia Boy and Sweets ready to take over their area, and I don't want my cash flow interrupted."

Spade nodded that he understood.

With that done, Derrick walked towards his personal elevator with two men in front, two men behind, and Spade at his side.

"Gentlemen, I am restructuring the organization tonight. If you have any aspirations about advancement, I'd like to hear it," Derrick finished as the elevator door closed.

CRUSH Groove

A group of neighborhood kids were playing street football as they dodged in and out of parked cars while oncoming traffic passed. An older couple crossed the neighborhood street with the flow of traffic holding hands. Everett drove behind the first black SUV that had its lights flashing without the sirens. The person of interest was highly volatile with unpredictability. Everett had underestimated Derrick Crusher once.

Travis held onto the door handle as they weaved in and out of traffic, gripping it as the vehicles slowed to allow the elderly couple to exit the street.

"One time...One time!" was yelled loudly from one corner to the next from various people watching the police vehicles advance.

"So much for that," Cole said to no one in particular.

"What's that? Travis asked as his body was jerked backwards as Everett pressed down to accelerate.

"The element of surprise, T," Vania answered as her body was pressed into the door frame.

The speed of the neighborhood shifted. Groups that had been congregating for criminal activity fled in separate directions, and others followed the path of law enforcement with their eyes.

"Stay sharp," Everett said loudly and with intent as he pressed on the brakes abruptly, and he put the vehicle in park and exited to meet the first line of officers approaching the home.

Parents called out to their children who were slow to react, more curious to know what was going on.

"Get inside." Vania motioned with her head to a bystander who had pulled out their cell phone to video record.

Cole was on Everett's six as he approached and banged on the door.

"Columbus Police, we have an arrest warrant for Derrick Crusher. Open the door, or we will break it down!" Everett stood to the side of the front door and Cole on the other. Travis and Vania took cover while maintaining a line of sight on the front door.

Everett nodded and an officer holding a small battering ram approached the door.

"Hold on, hold on now." A woman opened the door with her hands up.

"Crush hasn't been here in over a year, and I don't know where he is, and unless you want me to sue y'all dumbasses, take that arrest warrant and shove it up your ass." She rolled her neck and her eyes in unison.

Everett motioned to an officer to secure her before the team entered to search for Derrick and to secure the premises.

"This is a violation. That warrant doesn't allow for third party access. I own this house and you violated my rights. I want everyone's name and badge..."

Cole had had enough of her and decided to cut her off.

"Yeah, we know, you're going to sue us. In the meantime, why don't you tell us where he is? Save the city from being blasted with his fury. We have a witness; there is no way he escapes this. Maybe the city can though." Cole stood up and walked away to let her have a moment to think.

"Where did the intel on this come from?" Cole asked rhetorically as he passed Everett to exit the home.

Everett looked around the home for a second time. Nothing was out of place.

"There's nothing here." He relayed to Vania walking down the stairs and back into the living room.

Vania nodded toward Travis who was sitting with the woman identified as Sierra Carpenter. Travis was carrying a conversation with her.

"Thank you, I know how hard it is. I am truly sorry for your loss. Tell the family my condolences." Travis touched her shoulder and excused himself.

"What's that about T?" Vania asked before Everett had a chance.

Travis walked them outside and flagged Cole down.

"She grew up with my brother. Smart woman who just got caught up with the wrong person at a time she was lost. She says she hasn't seen him since he put a marker on her cousin a year ago." Travis hesitated as he got strange looks from each of them.

"Long story, but she did give something. His organization is falling apart from the inside out. Two lieutenants, dead and a civilian woman who was caught in the middle."

"We are no closer to knowing his location. V.A. can you reach out to your old unit and find out the structure of his organization? With any luck, one of his employees isn't feeling secure with his boss on a rampage. Travis find out everything you can about this so called 'innocent woman.' If she was affiliated with Crush, she couldn't be too far removed from the game. Let's go."

They followed him back to the vehicle and got in.

"I'm glad no one had to discharge their weapon." Travis spoke to no one in particular.

Everett pulled out into the street before looking in the rearview mirror.

"Travis, don't make your approach so shallow next time."

Cole nodded his head in agreement.

CRUSH *Groove*

The elevator door seemed to open much more slowly than usual. Everett and Cole walked straight into Captain

Montgomery's office and closed the door.

"Out of the frying pan and into the damn oven. Someone is trying to put me in my place. Thank God I still have honorable friends. Officer Early is being picked apart as we speak. His financials, his duty logs, the mileage on his vehicle, what the piece of shit ate for breakfast last week. He fed his informant the information to feed to the department." Captain Montgomery's agitation was front and center.

"If the warrant turns out we have problems, this won't end well...for us." Cole was just as worried as his boss.

Everett stood in the corner trying to piece together everything since learning Vania recognized both male victims as ranking members of Crusher's organization.

"Number one: I know that no one has been retaliated against for their deaths, and the footage from the neighbor's doorbell cameras puts him in the building which gives us more than enough standing. Who else is under investigation?" Everett didn't like feeling like he was playing defense, and he held no appreciation to the fact that his department had a mole in it.

"Early is the only one known for sure. For now, you and the team hold this close to the vest. You may imagine that there are forces trying to put pressure on us. Don't imagine what's real. Malcolm and Sheldon have something to share with you. Be careful." The captain opened the door to allow his senior detectives to leave.

"Oh, yeah, serious as serious is. This won't be good," Vania said lowly.

Cole walked past his desk and headed toward the stairwell. He didn't make eye contact with anyone as he reached for his cell phone and opened the door.

Everett walked out of the office, followed by the captain who stood in his doorway.

Everett nodded at Travis and Vania that it was time to go.

"Whoa, what was that about?" Travis asked as they waited on the elevator.

It was Captain Montgomery's voice that answered the young detective's question, addressing the remaining officers and detectives.

"Every last one of you, listen up! When the lives of my detectives are put in harm's way, I take no greater offense. There is a war brewing in this city in case none of you, 'professionals' can figure it out. We are the first and last line of defense, so there will be no bystanders. Don't come to work if your attitude is 'I'm just doing my job' to collect a paycheck. Do your damn job and clear your cases." Captain Montgomery walked back into his office, slamming his door, as Everett and his two younger team members stepped into the elevator, allowing the door to close behind them.

"Officer Early's bank account was flagged by Internal Affairs after large sums of cash had been deposited. They found out he's been working with Derrick Crusher's organization for the past seven years." Everett looked at both of them.

Travis showed disbelief on his face. Clarence Early had hung out with them on several occasions after work.

"Wow." Travis had no additional words.

Vania didn't show any emotion, but her words spoke volumes.

"We got set up and could've been ambushed earlier."

"Well, we weren't, only our team has this information, they have eyes on Early now." Everett added as the elevator door opened.

Cole, Sheldon, and Malcolm were congregated in the hallway, outside of the forensics lab.

"So, I was going over some of the findings we found in the murder cases against Crusher's organization. Some of them have been altered, slightly, but enough to create an error in any of our findings." Sheldon was visibly agitated.

"How can you be sure they were altered?" Everett asked Sheldon as he listened.

"I make sure I compile any evidence into a file on my

computer and then I upload it to my server. The file Malcolm has is the actual findings, and what Cole is holding onto is what Malcolm found on his desk."

"So, there's someone working against us in the lab too?" Travis posed the question to no one in particular.

"Okay, so let's assume that it's true. How can we find out who rolled the false report and then use them to root out this infestation?" Malcolm reached out for Cole to hand him the file he was holding.

"Can't we just run the video back and see who put it on your desk?" Vania posed the question.

"No, I mean, it's not that simple. The lab cameras are on the door and certain testing areas. Any completed file or result of test goes into one of three bins upon completion. They are then double checked and verified before being submitted..." Malcolm paused and looked upward.

"Plus, I made sure my office is not in line of sight of any camera angle."

"You can't be serious?" Everett was in disbelief.

"What happens in my office stays in my office." Malcolm replied flatly.

"We can make up a ghost file, feed a false narrative to the technicians that implicate Crush, and see where it takes us. Let them follow breadcrumbs back to us."

Sheldon had more emotion in his voice than usual. He was taking this personally.

"Yeah, let's get to it." Malcolm handed the files back to Sheldon and continued speaking with the four detectives.

"The file had to have been changed in the past two weeks. Don't trust anyone in this lab until we get to the bottom of this."

The door to the forensics department opened, and Veronica nearly bumped into Cole.

"Oh, man, I'm sorry. My first day back has been a little more difficult than I imagined. Why are you all huddled out here like a basketball team?"

No one said anything until Sheldon spoke up.

"Ms. Veronica someone is compromising our lab and our detectives. Our team is going to find out who it is." He was straight to the point. She had been gone for three weeks after her ordeal and wasn't included in the pool of suspects.

"Indeed." Malcolm added before walking with Sheldon back into the lab.

"We have some leads to follow. The sooner we get Crush off the street, the better." Everett walked away.

"Cole!" he called out to not make sure his partner knew he didn't approve of any interaction between him and Veronica.

Cole excused himself, leaving Travis, Vania, and Veronica in the hall.

"First day back and you are dumped into this." Vania hugged Veronica followed by Travis.

"I had cabin fever and was going stir crazy. It's strange though, I see things very differently now. Y'all got to excuse me though. I've been drinking coffee non-stop." She laughed as she walked towards the restroom.

"I don't think we need to have Everett or Cole in our shit right now, we still need to speak with the father of the female victim. I'm sure they're following up on a few leads that Sierra gave us this morning."

Travis and Vania walked up the stairs to the garage.

Everett and Cole were pulling out. Cole rolled his window down to address the younger team.

"Don't trust anyone outside of our team and make something happen."

CRUSH Groove

"Commissioner Grahl, welcome to Crush Groove, it's a little play on my name. I take it that this isn't a celebratory visit." Crusher motioned to The Commissioner to follow him onto his balcony.

Bowls with fruits occupied a table along with bottles of Champagne sitting on ice.

"The restaurant and dance club opened with a bang, we just pulled the plastic off the floors a few nights ago." Crusher poured more Champagne into his glass of OJ.

"I appreciate the misdirection on the raid. I can't have any hitches over these next couple of weeks. I'm going to hate to see you retire next year, we've had a beneficial relationship over the years.

The Commissioner poured himself a full glass of Champagne without the fruit juice.

"We do what we have to do Derrick. We are all in this together." The older man with gray hair sat down in one of the several chairs.

"So, what brings you to see me today, Pat?"

The commissioner sat forward.

"I've got word that a case I worked over two decades ago is being looked into again. I already put pressure on the department but the lab investigating with modern techniques is sure to find discrepancies."

"Say no more Pat, you know I keep my partners righteous. You stay clean and I stay clean." Crusher responded as an employee brought several dishes from the restaurant below.

"Jerk Lamb with wild rice, and Cajun Chicken and Sausage Gumbo as you ordered sir." A waiter pushed the large cart and made a plate for each.

"I need a message sent to whatever ADA is assigned to the Koiner case. I need that to go away." Crusher prayed before eating.

"God saves sinners too."

The conversation was short lived after eating. The commissioner exited the same way he entered. A remote access to the loft area. Crusher reiterated his position.

"Pat, I need that case to go away. I'll take care of your little problem. I've got to handle something too; I appreciate the intel on my 'video debut'."

The waiter removed the used dishes and cleaned the area before departing.

'Jack in the Box." Crusher called out, and one of his bodyguards appeared in the balcony arc.

"Yes sir." His voice was deep, as was his mahogany skin. Standing over six-foot four inches he weighed nearly three hundred pounds.

"Place a call to the Governor's man, I need a sit down with him. The commissioner may need to retire sooner than he intended, and make sure interference is ran with our people in the lab until I determine what's more beneficial to me." Crusher stood up and walked to the balcony. Fifteen years ago, he made a power play for control of the city. It was all about leverage and he found ways to compromise people. He found their weaknesses and exploited them.

CRUSH Groove

"Why the fuck do you all keep showing up at my door unannounced. Call me first, y'all both got cell phones and how either of y'all know I ain't have company?" Turtle walked away from the front door to allow Everett and Cole entrance to his home.

The place was cleaner than the last time they had paid him a visit during the child abduction investigation. The hardwood floor was swept and mopped. He had new furniture and a 65" flat screen television mounted on his wall.

"Who the hell did you rob?" Cole walked into the living room.

"Always think somebody is up to no good, don't you? Well, I got a real job now and I'm part of a union." Turtle sat down in his recliner and motioned for the partners to get to the reason why they came.

"A real job, that's good, really good. You're smarter

than people give you credit for." Everett paused as he walked back to the front door.

"What have you heard about anything going down with Derrick Crusher and his crew?" Everett returned to the sofa and sat down, leaving Cole standing in front of the television set.

Turtle leaned forward and pulled a blunt from his ashtray. He lit it and sat back in his recliner.

"I can't tell you much about Crush that you already don't know. Smart, and a ruthless psychopath. I heard he's been restructuring his organization." Turtle coughed from inhaling too much smoke.

"We know this already." Everett said.

"Just because I have a job paying me twenty dollars an hour now, that don't mean y'all get a discount. That little chump change you threw me last time..." Turtle coughed again and shook his head to indicate that it wasn't enough.

"Become a confidential CI and we can get you paid the right way." Cole spoke up.

"My name ain't going nowhere near y'all's police records. You and you are in here asking about someone who owns some of y'all police. This cat is too smart and has too many people protecting him." Turtle ashed his blunt.

Everett reached into his pocket and pulled out his

wallet. He understood the motivating factors for Turtle. Safety first and then cash.

"I have two hundred dollars in my hand. It can be yours, but we need some names or locations, that we don't already know. We have a witness that will testify against him and other evidence that will stick. So, what do you know?" Everett put the money on the small table.

Turtle reached for the cash, but Everett slammed his hand down on top of the money.

"Earn it."

Turtle stood up and paced his front room. He knew something but wasn't ready to share it exactly yet.

"Look, nobody likes Crush, they just fear him. Including me." He pushed past Cole and walked into the kitchen. He opened his refrigerator and pulled out a forty-ounce of Old English Malt Liquor. He twisted the cap off and took a big gulp.

"Crush has been inching new territory around the city, breaking peace accords with everyone. Word is, those who don't get on board...get ghosted. I can't be sure, but he played your little three car formation..." he sat down and continued.

"Everything gets around, and when the boys in blue fail, everybody know it." Turtle took another sip of malt liquor and then lit his blunt again.

Everett took the money off the table.

"Wait...slow down, slow down. You two make me feel so inexpensive."

"You are cheap, now stop fucking around." Cole was becoming irritated playing along with his antics.

"The last thing I heard about Crush is that he is laying low in the cut; some apartments he has some soldiers moving work out of. They can smell cops from a mile away."

"What apartments?" Everett sat forward as he waited on an answer.

"Buckeye Towers." Turtle took another hit from his blunt.

Cole sat down next to Everett.

Buckeye Towers was not a trap house, but a trap community. Derrick Crusher made his bones bending the community to his will. He had eliminated his competition through force, or whatever means necessary.

"Shit." Cole said.

"You damn right, shit. Rumor has it, that he's making a major move." Turtle agreed with him.

Everett stared off in the distance before standing from the sofa. He leaned forward and took forty dollars from the two hundred.

"Whoa, we had a deal." Turtle sat forward and took hold of the cash leftover.

"That's the fee for being so brand new, and also for not giving you a citation for the cannabis."

"I've got my medical marijuana card, and you know that." Turtle said before hitting his blunt again and exhaling it in their direction.

"Yeah, we remember, but in Ohio, you can't smoke flower yet. Take the win Turtle." Cole said as he followed Everett back to the car.

Once inside their vehicle, Everett relayed to his partner how they would keep Derrick's possible location a secret from everyone except those on his team. Vice would need to confirm the information and then they could move on him.

"We are going to have to be quiet about this. I will tell the captain in person and let him find out how accurate Turtle's information is. If confirmed, we can't roll up in there like we did earlier." He pulled out onto the neighborhood street watching as a mother carried her child in one arm and bags of groceries in the other.

Cole couldn't help but think back to Dallas and Chicago. After earning his bachelor's degree in Criminal Justice from the University of California he returned home to Dallas and joined the force. Cole established himself and then moved to Chicago for his sister's well-being.

Their parents had not approved of her same sex relationship. Wherever he traveled, he saw the struggle of survival imbued in the fabric of each city.

"The struggle never dies," he mumbled, staring out into the city.

CRUSH *Groove*

Sheldon had generated a false report and findings that led to evidence mounting up against Crusher. Malcolm falsified sample kits and left them out at different stations sporadically throughout the day.

"Your first day back after a traumatic ordeal, and it doesn't seem like you've skipped a beat," Malcolm said as he approached Veronica's station. He spoke loudly enough for others to overhear him.

"These need to be input into the system. This Crusher dude is going away for a long time." Malcolm winked at Veronica.

"Thank you, sir. The lab feels more like home to me. I will lay the file on your desk once I'm done sequencing the remaining DNA sample."

"Good, good. With all this evidence and the witness, we are going to make our streets much safer." Malcolm touched Veronica on the shoulder and walked to speak with Sheldon.

"Hey."

"Hey. The trap has been set. I have a meeting with this asshat that's been trying to cut our budget. I'm going to play nice for as long as I can, but I have no idea why he wants to cut our legs out from under us. The additional funding I've asked for is to modernize our lab. I am taking off, but call me with any updates." Malcolm made one more visit to his office. He sat down and played on his computer and then headed out the lab.

Everything seemed to be going like any other day in the lab. Tests were being run on various cases; some technicians had taken off already as they had been in since the crack of dawn.

"Veronica, you want to grab a bite really quick?'

The voice startled her, and she nearly dropped the glass beaker onto the countertop.

"Shit, if any of this stuff spills; that would not be a good thing." She made eye contact with Yari who had entered without her seeing.

"I am hungry, been on a coffee diet since I woke up." She slipped her gloves off, discarded them in a waste basket before hugging her friend.

"I have to check with Sheldon, we have some things we are trying to figure out and Malcolm's cracking the whip." She was interrupted by an older lab technician she had learned a great deal from. He was a balding man, still holding onto the last bit of hair as it was shaped like a half oval.

"If you're grabbing something, will you bring me a sandwich back?"

"Hey, Gene, what's up?" Yari shook the older man's hand.

"Please, get some meat on her bones. Here's thirty dollars for wherever you go. Just add extra mustard on my sammich... Keep the change." He paused as he chuckled.

"Has Sheldon been kinda uptight today? I mean, more than normal uptight. Let me finish this work on the computer so I can enjoy my food when you get back. Good seeing you Agent." He walked away putting his wallet back into his front pant pocket.

"I just got lunch paid for, yeah! You are my good luck charm." Veronica removed her lab coat and placed it over the chair to the station she worked.

"I'm thinking..." Yari started to speak.

"Corn beef sandwiches from Danny's Deli. It's Friday. What else have you eaten at lunch on a Friday since I've known you. Hello, everybody knows, even Gene knows." They laughed together making their way out of the lab.

Sheldon watched them leave and went back to acting like he was busy running tests, but his attention was on any behavior that seemed unusual from the remaining lot. The bait had been cast, and like fishing, he waited until someone was caught on the hook.

CRUSH Groove

Vania wove in and out of traffic safely after visiting the family of the two male victims. Each of their rap sheets were quite extensive. They had been with Derrick Crusher since grade school. Loyalty was best known from action accumulated over time, and for almost two decades, they had been family. Now both were dead. They were found murdered at the home of the innocent woman. The deceased woman was now a primary factor in the multiple homicide investigations.

"This cycle is cruel," Vania said as they passed run down homes. Some boarded up, were being used by squatters. Other homes abandoned, becoming eyesores to a beaten down community.

"It's grimy. It wears me down because so many gifted people get lost in everyday survival. I hope her parents have something that can be of use." Travis sat back and stared out of the window. The drive from the east side of Columbus to Worthington, Ohio would take time, and he was still thinking about Sierra.

She was older than he was. A scholar athlete with offers to any college, she wanted to attend for free.

Friends with his older brother and Rafi, she had become like a sister to him. Rafi always crushed on her, but back then he was still breaking his bones for the game. A terrible car accident took the lives of her parents. Shortly after, Derrick Crusher came into her life.

"Suburban parents are just as clueless as city parents," Vania said out loud as she exited the highway.

The difference was night and day from the neighborhood they had just left. Single standing homes had their lawns properly manicured. The houses separated with nearly half an acre in between. Vania found the address and pulled into a long driveway before pressing the ignition off.

"Let's keep it simple," Travis said as he closed his car door behind him.

"Simple it is." Vania walked ahead of Travis and pressed the doorbell.

The cobblestone pavement had recently been redone and from the smell, mulch recently laid. A jungle gym could be seen in the distance within a perimeter that separated them from the neighbors.

Vania rang the bell a second time as the front door opened.

A very fit, dark-skinned woman opened the door and stared at the younger pair.

"Can I help you?'

Travis had already removed his badge from under his shirt.

"Travis White and Vania Aguilar. Columbus Police, we had a few follow-up questions, is now a good time?"

Mrs. Miller took a deep breath and allowed them into her home. The open foyer was large with the living room sitting off to the left of the entrance. Deep wood floors frequented the house, with a merlot area rug sitting in the middle of an arrangement of cocoa brown furniture.

"Honey, who was it?"

Her husband walked from an area in the rear of the house and was surprised to see people inside the home.

"John, these are detectives. They have some questions about Kenya."

He greeted them and motioned them to have a seat.

Travis took out a small notepad while Vania gave condolences.

"We can't know the depth of your loss, and I can't imagine the pain. Some of the questions we need to ask may be uncomfortable, but we have to ask them." Vania ended at that and waited until she saw that both parents understood. She then continued.

"Were there any changes in behavior that stood out to

you? Anything that you can think of that seemed odd?" Vania finished the questions with her eyebrows raised.

Mr. Miller shook his head no, but it was his wife that spoke up.

"Kenya wanted to be part of the crowd. She thought suburban life lacked authenticity, and everything came easy. We tried to protect her from those things we had to fight to earn."

Her husband took her by the hand to lend her support.

"Some of the associates she hung around, we have confirmed were part of an unsavory bunch. Can you tell us if she had financial problems?" Travis asked.

Mr. Miller stood up and walked out of the living room to return with a manila folder in his hand.

"This is a printout from her financial accounts. We taught her fiscal responsibility but these withdrawals..." Mr. Miller paused as he laid the folder out in front of Vania and Travis.

"These two withdrawals of seventy-five hundred a piece, three days before she was murdered. It don't make sense. Why would she need fifteen thousand dollars?"

Vania kept listening to Mr. Miller as Travis looked deeper into the financial records. He saw that every month, the same amount had been withdrawn and was then deposited back exactly seven days later. For, every fifteen-thousand dollars taken out, it was replaced with a deposit of twenty-two thousand dollars.

"We know that she was starting to do promotional events. Could she have been using it for that? Honestly, we have no idea what she was doing with her money." Mrs. Miller was becoming emotional the longer the interview took.

"Do you have any names or contact information from the vendors or establishments she used?" Travis saw the numbers clearly. He knew fifteen thousand was roughly the cost a kilo of cocaine was sold to those with good connections, and that could be flipped for a much higher price after it had been cut with an additive. Checking with Kenya's contacts would verify either she was legitimately promoting events around the city, or secretly she had gotten into business with one of Derrick Crusher's Lieutenants found killed with her.

"Mrs. Miller! Mr. Miller, we thank you for your time, and we will continue to follow each lead until an arrest is made." Vania stood up from the couch.

"Can we take these? I think it can help us with the investigation." Travis looked across at Mr. Miller who shook his head affirmatively.

A loud crash was heard coming from another portion of the house. The sound of glass breaking startled everyone.

Travis and Vania looked at each other and were about to respond when a girl's voice was heard cursing profusely.

"Egypt watch your language and clean up whatever you broke!" Mrs. Miller excused herself to attend to their younger daughter.

"She's been taking it hard, really hard," Mr. Miller added before walking the detectives to the door.

"I don't care what you do to bring my child's murderer to justice. Whatever you need from us, you have it. Now, if you excuse me while I try to keep my family together."

Travis walked out first, followed by Vania.

When they sat back in the car, they had concluded that Kenya might have been a music promoter, but they were certain she had gotten into the business of cocaine.

CRUSH *Groove*

Saturday came and went. Everett and the team pressed on every lead to find Derrick but kept coming to a dead end. After studying Kenya's financial records, along with her cell phone texts and call logs, a pattern emerged.

"My contact in Vice says there is a shipment coming in on Monday of next week, but they don't have a lock yet. Derrick doesn't make mistakes like this, but it seems that when he killed his soldiers, he lost more than he gained,"

Vania said as she and Cole stared at the case board.

"We will move on him as soon as we get a hit. I'll stick around a little longer. We have this Crusher case to deal with, but we still have the thing in forensics." Everett paused as Travis sat down at his desk and turned his computer on.

"Travis don't touch anything on your desk until Monday. Vania if your contacts in Vice get a lead, make sure you call it in to me or Cole."

The elevator door opening drew their attention. Two uniformed officers were hauling a handcuffed woman to Detective Jack's desk, but the voice of another woman took Cole by surprise.

"How would I know that you would have him working on a Saturday? You both need to get a life."

The physical similarities were uncanny between the two.

"Mandy, I was just giving him the day off tomorrow but now that you're here," Everett said as he hugged Cole's sister.

Cole hugged her after Everett and then introduced the other two members to his sister.

"What are you doing back so soon? I didn't think you were coming until next week," Cole said with excitement in his voice.

"Big brother I do what I want..." She paused.

"Actually, I had to return for a consult with a client in Indianapolis yesterday, that extended into today. Instead of driving back to Chicago, to an empty house, I came to give you shit. The next thirty-six hours, I'll be tied up, so I checked into a hotel for the weekend. That should give you enough time to make up the guest bed and clean your place before I get there."

"Wow, Cole. You're at a loss for words," Vania said with a smirk on her face.

"I do have time to grab dinner. Everett I'm treating and you won't be telling me no. Your work will be sitting right there when you get back," Mandy said as she positioned herself in front of Everett's computer.

"That is really sound advice." Travis found it amusing.

"You two, can join us. If you have survived these two for this long, you are family too. I'd love to get to know you."

Both declined the offer but promised to accept any in the future. The fact of the matter, the team had gone nearly forty-eight hours straight and needed to rest.

"I made reservations for Hyde Park on High St. for eight o'clock. We have thirty minutes to spare."

The energy had lightened the moment Cole's sister stepped off the elevator. It was a much-needed change of pace.

"You two take off and rest." Mandy motioned to Travis and Vania who smiled and walked away.

"Dismissed!" Cole called out.

The conversation was filled with laughter and genuineness and Travis thought about his family as the elevator door closed.

"Hey, you want to go to church with me and my family tomorrow?" he asked after pressing the down button.

"Thanks for the offer, but no. I will be sleeping in."

CRUSH Groove

Travis had fallen asleep not long after he got home and woke the next morning still feeling tired. He picked his mother and nephews up for church and now he listened attentively to the sermon.

"The Lord is never on our time. We try to put God in a box and pull Him out when we need something, but that ain't the way it works. It works the way He wants it to work in His time." Pastor Bucknell was directing his sermon with passion. He walked up and down the aisles of the church. The deep emerald colored carpet seemed to make his feet float with each step he took.

Travis sat in one of the first few rows alongside his

mother and nephews. He took the cell phone from one of them after watching him text repeatedly as the Sunday Service went on.

"Darius, you can get this back after brunch, and if you say anything it won't be until I decide. Show some respect in the House of The Lord." Travis whispered lowly to not cause any unwanted attention.

Darius looked at his brother Albert who simply shook his head.

"You should've known better," Albert said before standing to join in the spiritual celebration.

Travis' mother had watched without saying a word. She was grateful Travis was playing the role of both uncle and father figure. She had come to many revelations over the years after her husband and son had been incarcerated. One was that if her grandchildren were going to have a better chance at life, they needed to spend as much time as possible being influenced by Travis.

"I'm sorry, Unc, this pretty little thing..." Darius was attempting to apologize, but Albert bumping him in the leg told him to let it go.

As service ended, Travis' mother spoke with a few members of the activity board. He and his nephews waited patiently in the foyer of the church.

"What's up, detective?" His friend Rafi from the

neighborhood walked up to him and gave him some dap. He punched the teenage nephews in the shoulders.

"Y'all staying strong?" he asked before pulling Travis to the side.

"I was thinking about some of the crazy shit we talked about growing up, giving back to the community. I want to open a community center to help with after school latch keys and tutoring, you know stuff like that."

"Is this 'center' going to be legitimate? Running D out of it isn't going to work, not on my watch." Travis made sure his friend understood that this was the non-starter.

"What? Man, get out of here. Hell, nah, I said the way we talked about giving back. Look I hustle, because I have to. Because if I'm not in the game our hood would be overrun with people only taking. Look, hit me up this week. I want to run some numbers by you before speaking with Pastor Bucknell." He finished before greeting Travis's mother.

"Hey, Mama White."

"Rafi, your mother, and I will be heading up pastor's birthday celebration. You and Travis will need to pick some items up for us."

Travis cell phone went off with a message that he was needed immediately at the lab.

"Okay, Mom, we have to get out of here, so I need to

drop you guys off; I've got to meet up with my team."
Travis' mother was not ready to leave, she still had
business to attend to.

"I need another thirty minutes with the committee
Travis..."

"Mama White, I can drop you and the boys off when
you are ready to leave. I assume my mom will be with you
for the next thirty-minutes. I can take the boys to pick up
food," Rafi offered.

His mother agreed, hugged Travis goodbye and
disappeared back into the church.

"Okay, Mom, I love you, and y'all better not cause any
problems." Travis nodded at his nephews before giving
dap to his friend.

"I know you don't take chances..." Travis was
interrupted before he finished.

"I don't ride dirty fool." Rafi pulled away and turned to
face the younger boys.

"Alright, alright, alright, what we gon get to eat little
men. What y'all like?"

Travis shook his head up and down before walking
away. He trusted Rafi with his family. Truth of the matter
was, without Rafi pushing him to stay away from hustling
and to do something better with his life, he could have
ended up in a very different place

His phone rang as he walked across Cleveland Avenue toward his parked vehicle.

"Travis White," he answered.

"Travis, it's Yari." There was a pause on the line

"Sorry, things are a little hectic right now. Listen carefully though. When you go to the lab, speak with Veronica directly. Please be discreet, very discreet. I have to go, but I'll get in touch with you later."

The phone line went dead.

Travis wasn't certain what Yari meant, or how she even knew he had been summoned to the lab.

He opened his car door, sat down, and started the ignition. For some reason, he knew "Easy like a Sunday Morning" was not going to be the theme song of the day.

Crush Groove

"That omelet was so good; your mom would have loved it too." Vania's roommate was standing in the kitchen at the sink rinsing off her plate.

Vania was pouring a second cup of coffee and wiping down the Keurig Coffee Maker.

"No, she would say. Mija, too much of this or too much of that..." Vania hesitated as her cat ran across her legs.

"Most of the time she was right. She's the only woman who can insult me with a compliment." They both laughed.

"I filled her bowl last night," Vania's roommate said as the cat purred and meowed as if she had something to say.

"Candy said to mind your own business auntie." Vania walked into the living room and sat down.

Her roommate followed behind.

"So, I watched one more episode of Star Trek Discovery, but I'll watch it again with you. I don't want to do anything but sit on this couch and do absolutely nothing today."

"You're not going to train at all today?" her roommate asked.

"I have no desire to spend the one day I have off rolling around on a mat. Truth be told, I'd rather do that than chasing murderers, but I like helping people." Vania leaned forward to scratch her foot.

"Woman, you like seeing the guilty realize they've been caught by you. Stop playing." Her roommate laughed and walked down the hall to her bedroom.

"The same way you like stitching people up." Vania laughed as she said it.

The theme music to the program was beginning when

there was a knock on the door.

"I got it, I got it," her roommate said as she walked quickly to the door with a five-dollar bill in her hand.

Vania leaned back over her chair to see who was at the door.

"This is for you." Her roommate handed a college aged male the money for delivering her items from the grocery store.

"Wow." Vania shook her head like she was shocked.

"What? I didn't feel like going to the store. I'm cooking Sunday dinner. You should invite Travis, I'm sure he likes to eat, and after spending the night with him at the hospital, he's much more interesting than you let on," she said as she carried three bags of groceries into their kitchen.

Vania had an inclination that her roommate was intrigued with Travis. After all, he was intelligent and trustworthy, and although Vania didn't look at him in that way, she could understand why her roommate and ex-boyfriend's sister found him attractive.

"You invite him. I'm not calling or texting anyone but my mother today. That's it." Vania slouched into her seat and went back to watching the science fiction futuristic show.

Candy purred in her lap and within minutes Vania had

dozed off.

Her roommate began cleaning collard greens and preparing them. She added water to a large pot and placed seasoned turkey legs in. She had learned to cook at the same time she had begun walking. After adding salt and pepper along with hot sauce and vinegar, she turned the heat on high.

Peeling and cutting potatoes for the garlic mashed potatoes didn't take long.

She thought about inviting Travis but hesitated. Instead, she removed three steaks from the refrigerator and placed them in a garlic marinade, before covering to put back in the refrigerator.

A grin traced across her lips realizing that in her day-to-day role, she made split second decisions on patients but couldn't decide on a dinner guest.

She grabbed her phone and texted Travis, as Vania's phone rang waking her.

"What's up, T?" She paused as Travis responded.

"On our day off and it's Sunday," she added.

Her expression changed and she sat more attentive.

"Okay, I'll be there within the hour, I need to shower and change." Vania hung up and disappeared into her room.

When she returned, she was dressed in all black and bullet proof vest. She had guns on both hips.

"What the fuck?" her roommate questioned her with concern in her voice.

"The three dead bodies from last week have a name associated with them and we have info on a person of interest. A retaliation early in the morning, has added two more bodies to the total. We need to stop this before it sparks a new war on territory." Vania grabbed two 20oz bottles of Pepsi from the refrigerator.

Her roommate looked even more confused.

"I'm trying to keep more bodies out of your operating rooms."

Vania put on a black hoodie and grabbed her keys. She picked her cellphone off the coffee table and headed for the door.

"Stay safe!" her roommate called out.

"I will, and you need to add more hot sauce and salt to that water." She looked over her shoulder allowing the door to close before her roommate could respond.

Crush Groove

The sheets hung halfway off the bed, and a few pillows had been thrown onto the floor. Cole lay in bed staring down at his right wrist. He was handcuffed to the wrist of a buzz cut woman with piercing blue eyes. She reached over and kissed him.

His head shifted to his left wrist as it was also cuffed. His lips met the mouth of her as well.

"Detective Cole Kennedy, you only posted half of your bail money last night. I believe you owe us."

Rachel paused as she looked across his chest to find the other woman's eyes.

"What do you think Ally? Another session should satisfy his debt," Rachel finished.

"I think two more session will satisfy my appetite," Cole answered.

"We didn't give you permission to speak Cole." Rachel slid over his body and kissed Ally.

"No, we did not," the buzz cut woman added.

Cole's ringtone went off that told him Everett was on the other line.

"Shit, shit, shit he has the absolute worst timing," Cole said as he set up in the bed.

"Can you grab my phone?" Cole nodded toward his phone laying on their mahogany dresser.

"No, we are going to have to work together," Ally

replied as she laughed loudly. Rachel joined in.

"This should be no problem as long as Cole can follow directions like last night."

Cole laughed along with them as they took turns getting off the bed.

Rachel grabbed his phone and accepted the call. She placed it to Cole's ear.

"Hey E, what's good?" Cole asked and listened.

"A review on a Sunday, in the forensic lab. Why do we have to..." Cole paused;

"Oh, okay, okay, I get it. I need to pick my gear up. Yes, I will have my head right partner. I'll be there in..." he hesitated as Rachel and Ally began kissing again.

"I'll be there within a couple of hours." Cole ended the call and was pulled back to the bed. Cole's ringer went off again from Everett calling.

Ally grabbed the keys to release the handcuffs from him.

"You owe us, Cole," Rachel said before kissing him again.

"Not to worry, like the Lannister's from Game of Thrones, I always pay my debt." He searched for his clothing that had been spread out over Rachel and Ally's home.

"I can make coffee," Rachel said as she walked naked to her kitchen, her breasts full, she had a carefree energy surrounding her.

"No time," Cole answered as Ally walked by him naked.

"There may not be enough time for pleasure... for you." Ally kissed Rachel's neck who had already pressed a button to brew a carafe.

"But you have time to take a coffee to go." Ally reached into a cupboard for a coffee mug.

Cole laced up his shoes and accepted the offer for coffee.

"Heavy cream and heavy sugar, just like you two." He winked at them.

CRUSH Groove

Everett was sitting in Malcolm's office when Vania walked in. Travis was staring at a file, as he stood in front of a white board looking at its contents.

A group of suits were checking the lab equipment not in use. A last-minute audit being done on a Sunday was meant as a message from someone Malcolm had pissed off. Luckily, he had a couple of contacts who gave him a heads up. For now, a full inspection could not be performed, and he hoped in the interim he could find out who was behind this violation.

"What's up with the suits?" Vania asked when she walked in.

"Not sure, Malcolm is dealing with it. We have a witness against Crusher, and we are waiting on the arrest warrant. There can be no mistakes." Everett was tense, and Vania could feel it.

"Sunday pickup," Vania said, as Travis walked into Malcolm's office to join them.

Everett looked at his watch and then his cell phone. His impatience couldn't be contained.

"He should've been here by now," Everett said to himself.

Cole walked in and made eye contact with Malcolm who nodded in the direction of his team.

Cole waved at Veronica, who acknowledged him with a nod.

"Travis, you still have on your church clothes, don't stand so close to me or we might catch fire." Cole paused before addressing the other two people present.

"Hey, partner, who woulda thunk on our day off we get to apprehend one of the biggest forces in our criminal underbelly, in his fortress at that. When's the briefing?" Cole asked.

From Travis and Vania's expression they had not been fully briefed yet.

"Can you take this seriously? Crusher got away with shooting at cops the last time he needed to be questioned. The arrest warrant should be in, check your weapons and be focused. No one ends up dead. That's not happening on my watch." Everett placed his hands on the top of his bullet proof vest.

"When's the squad being briefed?" Cole asked a second time as Everett walked away.

"Man, he's making me nervous," Vania said.

"You should be. It was one of Everett's first cases and a member of his team was shot. So, let's not fuck up." Cole walked out of the office followed by Vania.

Travis hung back and made his way to Veronica's station.

"Yari said you had something for me to look at." Travis approached her.

Veronica nodded toward a file that showed findings of the three murdered victims. Fingerprints showed that Rafi had been in Kenya's home at some point. It wasn't indicative that his friend had killed someone, only that he had been in the home where the bodies had been found.

"This, this is a lot to process." Travis had no idea what it meant.

"We haven't updated this yet, but Yari needed you to see this. I have to add this to the findings before end of business tomorrow." Veronica walked around her table to shield others from looking on.

"Can you give me forty-eight hours? Can you do that for me Veronica?" Travis met her eyes and waited.

Veronica squinted like she was calculating something in her head. She took a deep breath before replying.

"I can give you twenty-four hours maybe thirty-six tops. After that, I have to answer to either him or his boss." She allowed her eyes to scan the room to where Sheldon and Malcolm were speaking with a member of the audit team.

"I can't believe we are working on a Sunday," Veronica added.

"Welcome to the club. I need to gear up, today's suspect is the worst of the worst." Travis handed Veronica the file and walked out of the lab.

Crush Groove

The Buckeye Towers were a set of low-income housing apartments where many occupants worked under Crusher's organization. Derrick Crusher was verified to be occupying an entire floor, waiting for a delivery to arrive. This was the epicenter of his power, and as Cole and the two younger members listened to Everett's plan to apprehend Crusher, they knew there was no room for error.

"I want your teams to come in fast and hard on these two entrances." Everett pointed at a map which was projected onto a large screen.

"We will make it seem like we are rounding up felons, which should make scarce those surrounding the buildings." An older man of stature spoke up with leadership in his voice.

"Good, that's perfect Commander Rahker. While you guys provide deception, my team will enter here." Everett pointed to an emergency exit located at the back of the building. It wasn't connected to the three main units but close enough that the subterfuge had a good probability to work.

"We will make our way up this staircase and get the job done. Identify any threats and neutralize them but remember there will be civilians. Any questions?" Everett scanned the room to let his eyes rest on his team.

Captain Montgomery looked around the briefing room and understood how significant this moment was.

"I don't need to tell any of you the gravity of this move. Make it right and make it work." He walked out of the meeting, leaving the last bit to those commanding the teams.

"Team A, you will approach from the north and establish a perimeter. B Team, a full-frontal approach and identify yourself with warrants in hand. Those unwilling to comply will be forced to comply within the authority of the law. Extra ammo and stay sharp. You have fifteen minutes." Commander Rahker excused himself to have one final word with Captain Montgomery alone.

"Gentlemen and Ladies." Cole stepped to the side to let the Swat team leave.

"Close the door," Everett instructed Cole.

Everett then proceeded to go over the plan two additional times.

"We follow the plan. Derrick Crusher is the unpredictable factor in all of this. Like Commander said extra ammo, we leave in five minutes."

CRUSH Groove

The Swat vans surrounded the perimeter of Buckeye Towers. Everett's team could hear the members of swat on the communication earpieces provided. Those with outstanding warrants were being identified and apprehended. Those who were working the city block near the apartments had also been taken into custody.

The deception had worked so far, and as his team entered the rear of the stand-alone building, their senses were heightened.

Everett walked the first flight of stairs with his gun positioned and ready to fire. After quickly surveying the stairwell, he motioned with two fingers for Cole to bring up the rear. He made eye contact with Vania and motioned her to follow directly behind him. Then he signaled for Travis to move up.

A voice came through on the com system. "We've got another runner."

Everett walked up the second flight of stairs to stand opposite of Vania on the apartment door that Derrick Crusher had been confirmed. Travis moved to cover the hallway and that's when he noticed a door opening, and two men fleeing with black book bags on their back and guns in their hands.

One of the men saw Travis and took aim while the other closed the door behind him.

"Gun! Gun! Gun!" Travis yelled and aimed in return.

"Pop! Pop! Pop!" Three shots rang out quickly, and the two men dropped.

Cole moved up one level and Vania down the hall to check the vitals of both men.

She looked back toward her team and shook her head.

Everett grabbed Travis by the vest and looked him in

the eyes.

"I did what had to be done. If you hesitate you die."

Everett turned and banged on the apartment door.

"Derrick Crusher, we have a warrant for your arrest." Everett yelled loudly.

"Shit, shit, shit. Gun!" Cole yelled as a group of men were entering the building and making their way up the stairs.

Everett looked around, thinking quickly.

"V.A. no one gets up that staircase to outflank us. Travis go with her." Everett began kicking on the apartment door. He had no idea what lay on the other side but being sitting ducks was not an option.

He called over the com as he kicked the door for assistance, and that's when he heard the first volley of shots.

"Ain't none of y'all muthafuckas making it out alive!" the first voice called out as he ran up the stairs leading the charge.

Cole shot him in the head as he rounded the corner.

Bullets were returned but none could see where Cole was positioned. Everett moved up the final flight of stairs to look down the small gap.

"Where you think you going, huh?" Vania shot someone in the shoulder who then quickly retreated.

Another apartment door opened on the upper floor Everett had moved to on the stairs.

He saw the barrel of the AK-47 before the person emerged.

Everett shifted his body to hug the wall to not be seen. The shooter checked his right as he walked slowly out of the apartment door.

Everett had already taken aim, and as the gunman turned to check his left, Everett shot him in between his eyes.

"We could really use some help," he called out through his coms again.

Cole had fired more rounds but had to retreat to the second level as some more emboldened soldiers advanced.

"Reloading! Reloading!" Cole called out.

Travis ran to Cole's position and shot the next two men who turned the corner of the flight of stairs.

Vania maintained her position, but she could see another wave of gunmen.

Everett retrieved the assault rifle, checked the cartridge, and made it ready.

"V.A. on my six." Everett moved quickly down the front stairs, checking the corners.

"No one de can get in, is that understood!"

He then moved with haste toward the second entrance, stepping over the bodies lying in the hall.

"If any team can hear me, we need assistance."

"Cole, don't take your eye off that apartment door. Travis make sure no one else comes out on the third.

"Here they come!"

The sound of gunfire rang out, and bodies dropped.

The AK-47 was an assault rifle Everett had grown up with. As he let off one round and then another, those attempting to charge through the rear entrance thought again.

Travis shot downward through small space in between the flight of stairs.

Police sirens were heard as the shots being fired into the building slowed. Help had arrived.

Vania could see two officers down, and she moved down a level to return fire as other officers pulled them out of harm.

"Officer down! Officer down!" Cole heard the transmission in his coms. The large group that had rushed the building to protect Crusher were now engaged in a shoot-out with members of the task force.

The chaos had died down, and the police in battle gear kept a heavy presence.

Those who had tried to ambush the team were either dead, fled, or taken into custody.

"We came as soon as we could. We had a situation too." One of the squad leaders walked past the dead bodies in the building after checking on his wounded and fallen.

"Thanks for the assist." Everett watched Cole kicking the door to Derrick Crusher's apartment. The door had been reinforced.

"Grab the ram." The squad leader directed someone.

Everyone pointed their guns at the apartment door at the sounds of multiple locks being unfastened.

"Derrick Crusher, we have a warrant for your..." Cole began calling out and the door opened with a naked woman with Bose headphones laying on her neck. Standing behind her was Derrick Crusher, also naked with a pair of headphones.

"My bad fellas, we couldn't hear anything. We like to listen to Wu Tang when we bang, and you see we turn that shit *all* the way up." He started laughing.

"Read him his rights and put some clothes on him."
The swat leader directed members of his team.

They found his clothing and dressed him.

"Baby, call my lawyer. I'll be out in a couple of hours,
so make some mac and cheese and those collards. Use a
ham hock for the green beans. Instead of steak I want to
eat those pork chops. Do pigs eat pork?" He laughed again
as they hauled him out the apartment and down the stairs.

"I see someone is going to have to clean all this shit up.
Somebody is going to have to pay a heavy cost for this," he
said, seeing the bodies of those who had rushed to defend
him.

"It seems like a heavy price has already been paid,"
Everett said, watching him being led out.

Everett and his team walked out into scene
investigators wanting to ask questions. Everett kept
walking.

"We need a statement from you all!" a brunette
woman called out.

"Get it at the station," Cole said.

"I need your weapons before you leave and that's not
negotiable!" she yelled louder than previously.

Everett backtracked, released the magazine from his
weapon and ejected the round in the chamber.

The rest of the team did the same and then got into their vehicle and left.

CRUSH Groove

"The arrest warrant is solid and the evidence we have against your client is conclusive. The bullet found at the scene of the crime, the one that was spent from the chamber has a 100 percent match to his prints on file. The cell phone records of his former employees indicate that your client's cell phone was also pinging off the same tower, and to be exact, our forensics department has put it within twenty meters of where the bodies were found Mr. Jeffries." ADA Jefferson laid out a portion of her budding case.

Opposing counsel had scribbled down what had just been relayed. He adjusted his glasses and laid the ink pen on top of his legal pad.

"My client might accept that he touched ammunition after it was dropped from a box that he threw away after finding it. If I'm not mistaken, the building that those three unfortunate murders occurred in has several units, and it is possible that my client, by pure coincidence, could've been visiting a friend but that doesn't put him 'at the scene.' The shoot out that your detectives participated in was in no way attributed to my client. In fact, I'm sure your officers will testify to that account."

Commander Rahker watched with Everett behind the mirrored glass. It was not reassuring to hear Martin Jeffries rebut the ADA's claim.

"We have footage of him in the hallway from one of those ring doorbell systems, but we can't confirm he pulled the trigger." Cole shook his head and walked out of the room.

Travis' cell phone vibrated with a text message indicator. It was Yari with a sequence of question marks. Travis had forgotten about Rafi's connection.

"Soon." He messaged her back.

He understood he needed to have a conversation with Rafi and hoped that today would not be the day he had to arrest his best friend.

"Hey, I need to step out for an hour or so. Call me if you need me." He didn't go into detail with Vania, this was something he had to do on his own.

As he opened the door, Malcolm nearly knocked him over.

"Dammit, I'm not as quick as I used to be." Malcolm stepped aside and walked into the room after Travis left.

"We made progress," Malcolm said slowly, not sure if Commander Rahker was privileged to the secondary investigations happening.

"It's ok, he knows. His men are surveilling Early." Captain Montgomery relayed before turning down the speaker from the interview room.

"Gene, one of the technicians that has been here the longest. I readjusted the camera in my office to have a better look. I also ran a trace program that makes it possible for me to determine which employee added the final findings. Two of the files that we 'used' were altered by him."

Cole walked in with the team leader who saved them in the shootout.

"Commander, we intercepted the delivery. Over thirty kilos of cocaine and another haul of weapons.

Assault rifles, grenade launchers."

"Can we tie any of it back to him?" Captain Montgomery asked. He knew that getting a huge shipment of drugs and guns off the street was a success, but unless it could be used against Crusher, they were still in the same predicament.

"Where is Gene now?' Everett asked.

"Oh, he's still in the lab. I put him on a worthless task and put the fear of God in him not to leave until it was done." Malcolm shrugged his shoulders.

"Let's go get him. I have an idea." Everett and Malcolm exited to leave Vania with the Captain and Commander as the interview progressed. They turned the volume back up.

"These are some serious counts and all of them carry life without parole. Under the right conditions, the death penalty. I don't know.It really all depends on your client." ADA Jefferson pressed.

Derrick had been quiet but knowing most of the evidence was circumstantial except the bullet, he wanted to express his opinion.

"Here's what's going to happen. In the next six hours I'm going to be released. Within the following twenty-four hours, all of these charges will be dropped, and after that, we will decide on a dollar amount to lay on the city. Proof is hard to come by these days..." His voice trailed off as the door to the interview room opened.

Everett and Malcolm pulled Gene into the room acting like they didn't know it was occupied.

"Gene, thanks for telling us how it all goes down." Everett looked up at the two attorneys and then Derrick.

"Oh, I'm sorry. We didn't know." Malcolm made a genuine gesture like they made a mistake.

"Crusher, you know, Gene, this must be awkward." Everett finished and ushered Gene out of the room.

ADA Jefferson saw the shift in both client and counsel.

"Interesting. If you both will excuse me." She pushed her chair back from the table and left the room, walking into a perplexed Gene who was now hyper ventilating.

"Breathe...breathe Gene. Nice and easy." Malcolm offered advice.

"You... you guys have killed me and my family. You just sentenced us all to death." Gene tried to get up and leave.

"Sit down. You're going to answer some questions and depending on how truthful you are is how deep your deal might be. If you lie to me, I will charge you as an accomplice to everything Mr. Crusher will be charged with. I hope you understand the gravity of your dilemma." ADA Jefferson went straight to the point.

"Did you not hear me? He's going to kill me and my wife. You don't know. He's an evil man. Behind his wit and charm." Gene started to breathe sporadically again.

"Can you protect us? Can you protect me and my wife if I can give you concrete proof of all the crimes he committed for immunity and witness protection? Please." Gene pleaded.

ADA Jefferson could authorize this herself with the stakes so high.

"Let's see what you have to offer, and then we can..." she was interrupted.

"Here... here." Gene handed Everett a USB drive.

"Everything, everything I have ever done is on here. I'm sorry but he threatened my life, the life of my wife."

"Put him in number three," Captain Montgomery ordered.

"Am I under arrest?" Gene asked as he was being pulled away.

"Gene, shut up. Just shut up and answer questions." Malcolm shook his head in disappointment.

Everett had already walked to his desk to see what was on the USB.

Several folders were listed. Everett clicked on the Video file and clicked on one dated the day of the triple homicide.

A video played of Derrick Crusher being present when someone else pulled the trigger on all three homicides.

"Didn't we download all the contents of Kenya's laptop?" Everett asked.

Malcolm looked at the video and then checked a directory of the video.

"This video was transferred before the scrub," Malcolm mumbled.

"Why not take the computer and destroy it?" Cole asked.

"Because of something called 'the cloud.'

Cole and Everett looked at each other.

ADA Jefferson walked out of the room with Gene still sitting and over to Everett's desk.

Everett ran the video again.

"Send that to my email address right now." She excused herself and walked back into the interview room with Derrick and Attorney Jefferies. Everett caught up with her before the door closed and entered. He stood off away from the table.

ADA Jefferson sat down at the table slow and deliberate before pulling her laptop computer from her bag on the back of her chair.

She pulled up the video and turned her computer toward Derrick and his Attorney.

"Today has been a helluva day for you; a Sunday at that. This is supposed to be a rest day. Oh, wait it is... an arrest day," Everett said as he watched the blood drain from Derrick's face.

CRUSH *Groove*

Travis knocked on Rafi's door and waited.

A caramel complexioned woman came to the door and

stared at Travis. She had on light blue boy shorts and a white t-shirt.

"Pebbles, open the damn door! Don't be all funky and shit," Rafi said as he peeked around the corner.

"Well, I don't know this dude, to be honest he look like a cop," she said as she unlocked the door and disappeared into another portion of the home.

"He is a cop and the only real friend I got. Make me something to eat..." Rafi paused

"You want something?" he asked Travis who shook his head no.

"I want some steak and fries, with some Grape Kool-Aid." He gave his food request to Pebbles.

"You know your mom loves what you do, but she is worried about you, Travis. Your nephews got some skills with the flow too." Rafi walked through his living room and kitchen.

Pebbles was already rinsing the steak off.

"Give it that Jamaican touch, baby," Rafi added as he and Travis walked downstairs to his basement.

"I haven't been down here, since... shit, I can't even remember," Travis said as he touched the rail of a full-sized pool table. He took the white cue ball and pushed it across the red felt.

"So, what's up, T? I thought church would be the only time I saw you today." Rafi knew his friend and knew something was on his mind.

"Your prints were found at the scene of a triple homicide." Travis waited for a response.

Rafi smiled and walked to a homemade bar with six bar stools around it. He pulled out two rocks glasses before reaching back and pouring himself Hennessey and Travis the same amount of Everetton.

"You got time to play?" he asked, as he waited for Travis to take the brown liquid libation.

He began to rack the balls.

"Kenya, well, Kenya was one of my contacts, and I had just made a pick-up. She was cutting into Crush's market and using his Lieutenants to do it. I got what I could get out of it before the shit blew back on me. I didn't kill her or any of them. I'm not a killer... Really, you know this." He finished as Travis sipped his drink.

"I think I beat you last time, so it's my break," Rafi said as he set the cue ball on the table.

"When have you ever beat me at pool? You can break though because you need all the help you can get. Is it cool if I take you up on the offer for food?" Travis poured himself a heavier drink.

"Yeah, man, she already knows to make extra for my

family...." Rafi paused to look back at Travis before he broke.

"She knows who my family is fool."

CHAPTER TWO
We ALL Want Better

Malcolm walked his front yard with his two dogs. The morning frosts were soon to be done, and the beautiful wonders of nature would be springing to life. He still had a few hours before he had to meet Avery to bring him on board with his department. Malcolm knew the benefit the forensic department would have with Avery joining the team, more importantly it also would challenge Malcolm to keep up with trending technologies.

Malcolm's dogs started barking loudly before running toward a vehicle making its way up his long driveway.

"Come here, you big babies." Cole exited his driver side door and ran towards the dogs. They ran up to him before running away as he chased them.

"It's too early for you to have driven out here, so this must be good." Malcolm walked to Cole now patting both dogs.

"I was fifteen minutes down the road and knew you'd be awake…" Cole paused as he stood up.

"The woman I hooked up with last night doesn't have coffee, and she snores."

Malcolm laughed and walked back into his home with Cole on his heels.

"Well, thank God Cole Kennedy has a brother from another mother like me. I need to hop in the shower, coffee is… well, you know and please don't add sugar to the pot. I don't need diabetes." Malcolm left Cole to fend for himself.

He got a text message from the woman he had spent the night with asking why he left so early.

Cole spent a few moments making sure he chose the right words to not offend or create energy that was negative. In the end, he would see her again, but overnighters were off the list.

Cole turned the television on as the coffee brewed.

The morning news programming "The Jumpstart" started its' next topic. Cole smiled as the morning host covered the highlights of yesterday's news cycle.

Now, she didn't snore, he thought.

The dogs followed him around, expectant of a snack. Cole had been the dog sitter whenever Malcolm traveled to assist other forensic departments on high-profile cases from when they were mere pups.

"No, no." He snapped his fingers for both dogs to lay down.

"I don't know why they listen to you." Malcolm returned dressed. He poured coffee into a mug and sat down to watch the morning news with Cole.

"Captain Montgomery has been getting visits from brass lately. I wonder if he's finally getting looked at for advancement. He could've moved up years ago, but politics isn't really his thing." Cole turned the channel on the television.

"I thought she was 'green'." Malcolm mentioned about the newscaster. Cole shared every conquest with Malcolm. He was like an older brother to him and trusted him as much as he trusted Everett.

"Oh, she's definitely green," Cole responded in reference to his color grading ranking system he used when putting women in a hierarchy.

"You're such a slut." Malcolm laughed as he sent something from his cell phone to his printer in the home office.

"I'm offering a position to Avery." Malcolm retrieved the forms.

"Avery is the little tech guy you keep hidden?" Cole walked back into the kitchen and helped himself to a second cup of coffee.

"I'm not keeping him hidden. He's a unique individual, head strong like your partner, and I trust his work. He will be a valuable asset. I'm still working on his salary, but I don't think I can get the full amount." Malcolm shook his head as he looked over the forms for Avery.

"I wrote it into the new budget proposal, but there's been minor pushback as usual from all the budgeting committees."

"How much?" Cole asked.

"What?"

"How much you are you paying this Avery guy?" Cole clarified his question.

"The salary is fifty-thousand," Malcolm answered

flatly.

Cole laughed as he sat back down.

"Sheldon is second in charge in the lab, and he only makes eighty-thousand and that took him some time. How do you think your lab is going to…"

"Who cares… They get paid good, all things considered. When I tell you that 50k is a discount for him, I mean it. Avery has no idea the gift he possesses. He's smart, but the way he sees both the micro and macro elements along the same perspective that I do," Malcolm countered.

Cole shook his head and took his friend's word. He checked his watch.

"Alright, I gotta go. I need to beat Everett in today." Cole poured his coffee into a travel cup Malcolm had stacked in his pantry.

"Okay, you big babies come on, come on. Uncle Cole has something for you." He called for the dogs as he walked out of the living room patio door into Malcolm's front yard again.

The dogs followed him wagging their tails. Cole always brought them a treat and today was no different.

"Hey, sit, sit down." They listened and waited expectantly.

Cole pulled a Styrofoam container from his passenger

seat and opened the box.

"Here's a steak for you guys." He moved the meat towards the dogs slowly, making sure they remained patient.

"Good boy, good boy." They took the steaks and ran away.

"You didn't have to bring me to anything fancy." Avery shook his head in jest as he and Malcolm sat at a picnic table in front of and old mom and pop restaurant. The mini-food truck outside the establishment served those who wanted to pick up and go, after hours.

"Shut up and try the chicken tortilla soup." Malcolm was comfortable bringing the young tech wizard on board permanently, as opposed to the side consulting. Avery could follow direction, something he had to learn when he was younger.

"You're going to fit in. Just make sure you socialize every now and then with your coworkers. Get to know them, it will take time." Malcolm bit into fresh empanadas brought out by a server.

"Whew, this is the only place I take candidates that I like." He smacked his lips as he chewed the hot, meat pastry.

Avery pulled a shoe box from his book bag and slid it across the table.

"You ain't got enough money yet to be buying your boss gifts and shit.

Malcolm opened the box and pulled the black leather belt out.

"The shoes fit too. I made them specifically to be undetected from any scanning devices, but I can still get location. The small device is what I use. Try it out."

Malcolm looked inside at a small device with a miniature screen.

"Tracking device. I only have that and the prototype." Avery indicated that he needed to be careful with it.

"Batman and Robin." Malcolm shook his head in approval to his protégé.

"How many candidates have you brought here?" Avery changed the subject, dipping chips into freshly made salsa dip that nearly matched his cleanly shaved red hair.

"In nearly two decades of working in forensics, and the last fifteen leading this department, there have been three. My second in charge, Sheldon and two others, Veronica and Eugene," Malcolm said as a matter of fact.

Avery smirked and enjoyed the food.

"I'm still working with the departments budgeting guidelines, but I want to honest with you. I may not get the full funding." Malcolm checked his watch.

"I've got to get back to the lab." He paused to collect his refuse.

"The next time I say that, you'll be able to accompany me."

Malcolm shakes Avery's hand before walking back to his car.

AVERY

"Yo, M, thanks for the lunch again!"Avery called out.

"Thanks for the new bat gear." Malcolm nodded in return, got into his car, and drove away.

"Where's your partner?" Everett approached Travis without the younger detective seeing him. It startled him.

"Come on, boss, that military ninja stuff…" He shook his head before answering the question.

"She's not due in for another hour or so."

Everett checked his cell phone for the time.

"Why are you..." Everett looked closer and saw Travis was verifying paperwork.

"It never gets old does it, at least your consistent." Everett put his hand on Travis's shoulder and disappeared into the captain's office.

Travis went back to his paperwork. It wasn't until he heard Agent Yari and Veronica's voice that he looked up.

"Here T." Vania placed a plastic bag onto his desk.

"Don't say that I don't be thinking about you, ghetto nerd."

All three women laughed together.

"Street intelligent you mean." Travis smirked and thanked his partner for the food.

"Everett was asking about you, earlier." He relayed the message and opened his bag.

"Just what I needed." Travis unwrapped the sandwich and bit into the pickle accompanying it.

"They are the best. I have to get them at least once a week." Yari interjected about the lunch choice.

"Don't I know this." Veronica took her leave. She had two analysis she had been tasked with completing before the end of day.

"I'll see you tomorrow?" Yari asked Vania before

departing.

"I wouldn't miss it for the world."

Travis had half of his giant corn beef sandwich in hand.

"Miss what?" He moaned as he took a bite.

"A small house-warming party for her. She finally got the last bit of her renovations done..." Vania saw Cole and Everett walking onto the floor.

"I'd put that away before Cole wants the other half." She sat down at her desk and logged onto her computer.

"Uh, I don't think so... What you got in the bag?" Cole had seen Travis slip the bag into his desk.

"We could smell that as soon as we got off the elevator. I don't want any." Cole reassured the young detective.

"V.A., I'd rather be the one to tell you. The Annual City Ball is coming up next weekend and you will be on site." Everett watched the frown appear across her forehead.

"I didn't sign up for security detail or extra work, so how is that even possible?" she asked. Her tone became firmer, but she wasn't offensive.

"The cities who have Ambassadors will send representatives this year. The ambassador for the city of Cleveland has requested your presence. Not as security, but as his plus one."

Vania rolled her eyes.

"This is what my mom called me to tell me and I didn't get a chance to call her back. So, I have to dress up?" She sighed.

"Formal wear." Cole jabbed.

"I can't wait to see Queen of The South, I mean Columbus..." Travis laughed as loudly as the three women had earlier.

Captain Montgomery walked out of his office directly.

"Representative Stills was found murdered. You're on it and keep it quiet."

The mood changed instantly.

Representative Stills was beloved by his community. Championing latch key programs and family assistant programs, he was a rising star in the politics of the State of Ohio. He had recently gained a national following after his wife gave birth to triplets. His handlers used the momentum to test the waters for the office of mayor, or perhaps State Senator.

"Shit, there's going to be blowback either way it goes. Just make sure everything stays close to the vest." Captain Montgomery walked to a whiteboard and put the initials of the victim up with those assigned to his case.

"This investigation is going to test how thick your skin

is. Needless to say, many of his constituents aren't our biggest fans." Everett checked his cell phone before leading the team to the site of the murder.

The body was draped under a sheet, slumped forward in his desk chair. The elected official's office was an old space in the community he represented. The building, remodeled with modern day functionality at its center, was one of the projects Joseph Stills had taken on initially. Now, after six years, more than thirty percent of the run down and abandoned buildings were occupied, and a revitalization in the community created more wealth.

"Check the log in sheet for last week. Speak with everyone employed in this location. This investigation must be thorough." Everett and Cole left the b-team at the scene of the crime with Sheldon as he collected evidence.

"Two shots to the chest. He had to die quickly." Sheldon disappeared from the young detective's line of sight.

Vania had taken a video of all the names on the log in sheet, and Travis was speaking with employees who had not heard about the tragedy.

"He's dead." Multiple voices were heard outside of the

building, and a crowd began to form early in the morning.

"So much for quiet, Channel 10 and 6 are already on site." Vania approached Travis and pressed for more answers.

Vania and Travis commandeered office space and began interviewing the employees who had worked the previous day. Each of them were shocked that Representative Stills had been murdered. Those closest to him were hit the hardest.

"I thought we should have had security until the last person left the building, but he thought it was a waste of money. Wendy and the children." A brunette woman wearing navy blue slacks and chambray button down dress shirt was emotional. Her eyes were puffy.

"Zoey, there's a few reporters wanting a statement and Shepherd's not back from city hall. Can you do something with them?" An older woman approached.

"Yeah, just give me five minutes Ms. Burton." Zoey told the detectives if they had further questions, she would make herself available.

"Ms. Burton, since you're here we'd like to ask a few questions about Representative Stills..." Vania motioned her towards a seat.

Ms. Burton hesitated before she took the seat.

"Representative Stills was one of the best things to

happen to our ward in over twenty years. I worked with Representative Collins before he retired. I've seen ambitious people before and Joseph Stills was no different, except he was. This man rejected money from not so savory individuals when he needed it to maintain his last campaign. Instead, he dove into the community and found out that many people wanted change as much as he did." Ms. Burton answered multiple questions and that's when they found out that he had a heated discussion with the head of building enforcement.

"Yeah, that was a few weeks ago. Many people don't know the battles he fought for them. He turned away investors looking to buy property in his ward. He understood gentrification and the loss of cultural identity and presence built over decades," Ms. Burton finished.

Vania secured the name of the manager of building enforcement before excusing the older woman from the office.

"Zoey, excuse me. His campaign manager, Shepherd, is he..." Travis approached the young office manager with Vania at his side.

"I just spoke with him, and he's still in a meeting at city hall... The damn mayor didn't appreciate Joseph. He's already putting names into the pot for a replacement..." she paused to regain her composure.

"Wendy is not going to like it. She was the driving force

behind her husband. Even during her pregnancy, she and Shepherd held three-hour brainstorming sessions. Her babies, oh my god." Zoey shook her head, as another office worker called out her name that there was a call on line two from a national news organization.

"I can't handle all this shit."

Zoey's six words before departing showed her frustration.

"I don't think she's had time to process this." Vania watched her walk away.

"it's going to hit her like a ton of bricks when she lets it all sink in." Travis moved towards the exit with Vania at his side. They ignored the questions being thrown out by members of the media, before getting into their vehicle and driving off.

"It wasn't uncommon for him to work until all hours of the morning, but he would always call and update me." Wendy Stills was pumping breast milk for her three-month old triplets. The nanny was watching the babies in another room as they slept.

"I'm sorry but I have to do this, it's important to Joseph and I..." she hesitated because no matter how normal she wanted her life to remain, it was forever changed.

She finished her task and rehydrated with bottled water.

"Joseph did what was best for his community and someone took his life. What do I tell my children as they grow up? Who is going to teach them all the things he was supposed to?" Wendy walked them into the living room which overlooked a wooded backyard.

"Did your husband receive threats that garnered further investigation?" Everett knew the amount of hate mail those voted into office received. It was part of the job, but he also understood a few were viable from time to time.

Wendy's eyes were teary when she responded.

"We've had only two that were investigated but there was no credible threat of physical harm."

The grandfather clock struck the top of the hour and the chime rang five times.

"I can put you in touch with his campaign manager. He will have all of that information. Have you checked who was last to leave the headquarters last night? Did they see or hear anything?" Wendy was doing all she could to hold her emotions in.

"I should've made him come home last night."

Cole watched the nanny turn on the stove to heat water to be used to warm the infant's milk.

"What time did you speak with him last?" Cole understood how raw the emotions were for Wendy, but he had to ask these questions.

The nanny turned the stove off and placed three bottles of breast milk in the pot to warm.

Wendy reached for her phone to check her outbound call log.

"10:49pm. I wanted to tell him goodnight and to be safe. Please find out who killed my husband." Her voice contained pain and her eyes sadness, but dignity surrounded her.

"Mrs. Stills is there anything that seemed unusual with your husband lately, switch in routine; something that sticks out..." Everett paused as the nanny returned with one of the triplets for Wendy to feed.

"Honestly, I wouldn't be able to tell you. Shepherd handles Joseph's day to day." Her infant sucked in the milk through the nipple of the bottle. The child opened his eyes when he heard Everett's voice and quickly closed them as he sucked the milk down.

"We will do everything we can to find out who did this. Can you provide Shepherd's contact information and we can get out of your hair?" Everett watched the nanny walk back into the kitchen and write something down on a notepad. She returned and gave him the information requested.

"Thank you." He nodded as she exited and returned with another infant.

"If you don't have any further questions, please find whoever took their father away from them." She exchanged children with the nanny and told Everett and Cole to follow her to the exit.

"Joseph Stills was beloved by everyone in the neighborhood. Hell, when he stood up to The mayor's office, who defended those crooked cops, he won my vote." Ms. Tolls spoke out. Her blue jeans had holes in them, designed that way to signify fashion. Three bracelets dangled from one arm and an Apple Watch on the other.

"I wouldn't talk so loudly about crooked cops, after all, we are considered law enforcement." Veronica understood the subject was touchy.

"I'll speak my mind Veronica; good cops are the reason why I work as hard as I do. It's the dirty ones that I can't stand." Ms. Tolls finished and walked to a table with a centrifuge set up with a disgusted expression on her face.

Her mini afro was shaped perfectly and fit the strength of her face. Veronica believed she looked like a young Pam Grier.

"Veronica are you running the analysis on the bullet fragments pulled from the body?" Sheldon caught her attention. He held a clipboard in his hands awaiting her response.

"Already on it."

Her attention was drawn to Agent Yari who had entered, and now speaking with Ms. Tolls. She didn't seem as welcoming to her today.

"Yari." Veronica called out to get her friends attention.

"Damn, what's up with Ms. Tolls? She's usually all bubbly?"

The two women hugged briefly in greeting.

"She was a huge fan of Joseph Stills," Veronica answered.

"That's a shame, he was one of the better ones, not corrupted by politics, he stood his ground. I'm sure his position on gentrification didn't sit well with those developers who lost millions of dollars a couple of years ago." Yari spoke about the young State Representative with respect.

"Calling out members of the city government in bed

with criminals didn't make him any friends either."
Veronica saw Malcolm walk into the lab. He seemed
preoccupied.

Yari received a text from her boss to return to the
office immediately.

"I've been summoned. I've got wine and liquor for
tomorrow and a surprise." Yari winked and departed.

"Veronica." Ms. Tolls approached Veronica.

"Please tell Agent Yari that I know my emotions got the
best of me, and I apologize for being so short with her and
to you." She didn't wait for a response, instead she walked
into Malcolm's office. She spoke briefly with Malcolm
before removing her white lab coat to leave early for the
day.

"She is taking this really hard." Veronica thought, as
she got back into work for the next four hours.

A tap on her shoulder brought her attention back into
focus.

"You got in here at six am and it's after seven. I need
you to go home Veronica." Malcolm stood near her lab
table. His leather bag hung from his shoulder strap across
his body.

"I'm finishing up boss man, just waiting for the
preliminary results back from the bullet fragments."

Malcolm walked closer and slid her chair away from the desk. He scanned the material on the computer screen and saved it before closing the program.

"This will all be waiting for you tomorrow." Malcolm was using his authority to make sure she rested. He had seen many specialists quit, because they burned out. He knew Veronica was still sorting through bits of being stalked and spent more hours in the lab. Malcolm needed her to go home and rest.

He waited until she placed her lab coat on one of the hooks in their small personnel area.

"Sheldon, tomorrow after four hours, kick her out." He relayed the message so that the younger woman would not spend an entire shift working on a Saturday.

Sheldon shook his head in agreement and went back to scanning through a large binder.

"I will walk you to your car, you're ready?' Malcolm said it as more of a statement than question.

"Yeah, I'm ready and ..." she paused and called out to Sheldon.

"I appreciate you both more than you know, and I'm handling everything the best way I can. Spending time here and helping solve these open cases does more for me than sitting at home." She didn't wait for either man to respond as she walked out of the lab with Malcolm behind.

Everett and Cole had stayed up all night sorting through the financials of the deals that Representative Stills had on hold. Millions of dollars were in limbo simply because he found ways to slow down the progress of these projects. His constituents were tired of being victims of gentrification.

Shepherd Hall had spoken with the detectives over the phone late Friday evening and had made plans to come in and speak.

"He made a lot of families feel like they were being heard. The surrounding Wards have had sections of it bought up and improved. Prices of these newly developed homes and businesses price those who made the neighborhood up for over fifty years right out. Joseph was a staunch supporter of creating a better environment for those already living there." Shepherd was giving insight to what he knew why some may have held grudges.

"When people buy property, they can do what they want with it, and if someone finds value in it, what's wrong with that, capitalism right?" Cole wanted to dig a little deeper.

"That is true, but the city or state has always made it more difficult for those neighborhoods to receive money to help with the infrastructure. Why is his Ward and those surrounding it always last to get newer roads or money for revitalization of the city? Why have those areas where people have been pushed out, suddenly the recipient of money that could've gone to those wanting to make their neighborhood safe? Why do people believe that those surviving inflicted areas of crime and poverty shouldn't receive a helping hand?" Shepherd answered without pause.

Cole had not expected the retort and didn't have anything to push back with.

Everett was satisfied that Shepherd didn't have any tangible information to lead to the murderer being known.

They thanked him and walked him out of the interview room.

"Shepherd, really quick, who gains ground for his seat now that he's gone?" Everett had the question surface.

Shepherd stared upwards momentarily.

"The mayor backed Frances Hiller on the last ballot. Other than that, the Ward is up for grabs." Shepherd stepped onto the elevator and said his last goodbye.

"We are lucky that the news cycle caught this at the end of the day. Monday morning, we will have so many people up our ass." Cole knew how the media would take bits and pieces of information and run with it. Ratings were murder too.

"Yeah, I need to shower and regroup. I'm going to check and see if they have anything in the lab to help point us in a good direction. I'll call you if so." Everett walked back to his desk and grabbed his keys. Cole disappeared into another portion of the precinct.

Everett needed to pick his kids up by two o'clock. His parenting weekend started Friday, but Robbi had an event that she wanted them to attend with her. Everett had seen families destroyed by divorce. He had been called to homes of domestic violence. This would not be the legacy he left behind, even with his inability to open up to his ex-wife.

"Ms. Tolls, what are you doing here on a Saturday morning." Everett expected to see Sheldon.

The younger black woman nodded at Everett and shook his hand upon approach.

"Representative Stills needs justice. Our rising stars, those who can lead are snuffed out long before their time. The likes of Muhammad Ali and Dr. King; Malcolm X, those who knew sacrificing their life for the betterment of black folks are always cut short. Now Joseph Stills name is written on the same list."

Everett had known the popularity of Representative

Stills, but he didn't know the impact that he had across generations.

"Where is Sheldon?" Everett needed an update from him. Malcolm had flown to Dallas, Tx for a conference of leading forensic experts and he was the keynote speaker.

"He and Veronica walked to get coffee. He left the bullet fragment analysis over there." Ms. Tolls pointed to a desk as her bracelets clanged together.

"Thanks." Everett retrieved the file with copies of the findings.

Everett read over the report.

"Glock 17 pistol, so 9mm rounds. Angle of trajectory was head on." Everett spoke out loud.

"Sounds like he knew whoever it was. Who doesn't try to get out of the way of being shot? Seems like he was caught by surprise, huh?" Ms. Toll's questions were valid, and Everett had thought about those things too.

Everett had other questions that needed to be answered, but he knew his body needed to rest before his children arrived. He exited the lab and pressed the elevator button. As the doors opened, he saw Sheldon and Veronica walking from the opposite direction with coffee mugs and a store bag in hand.

He waved and walked into the elevator.

"That was more than fun and to have all the guys staring at us was boss. I mean, we are hot, but they started to record you two shooting." Veronica was feeling alive for the first time in months. Yari and Vania took her to the gun range. Veronica knew how to handle a handgun, but she was nowhere near the experts they were. Yari was hitting targets over 700 meters out with a custom-built Wilson Combat AR-10 Recon Tactical. It was her gift to herself when she was hired for the Human Trafficking squad over two years ago. The Vortex Viper Riflescope accessory was one of the best.

"Everett would kill to shoot your rifle." Vania was accurate with the sniper rifle up to 450 meters.

"This is our little secret. Boys will always try to outshine us." Yari placed her rifle case into the back of her Chevy Tahoe.

"Nice shooting ladies." An older couple walked across the lot, passing them to get to their car.

"I was a Calvary scout sniper and I tell you what, I was using my range finder, and at 600 meters your groupings were so tight." The husband had excitement in his voice. He asked to see her weapon and was amazed.

"We're trying out for the next roles of Charlie's Angels." Veronica laughed before Yari thanked the couple.

The ladies had already packed overnight bags for Yari's housewarming, and on the way back to her home they stopped and picked up dinner and snacks.

The house was an older house, built over sixty years ago. The 1-1/2 story Cape-Cod style home had a steep roofline, multi-paned windows, and wood siding. It was larger than most homes designed in the style, and this is what Yari had been attracted to when purchasing it. The hardwood floors and interior area still held authenticity.

Yari put close to forty thousand dollars into remodeling it over two years, and tonight she was celebrating with Vania and Veronica.

Her neighbors were spaced decently from each other and with the added privacy, she often walked her back property in a robe and slippers, completely hidden from the outside world.

In a sense, this is how she felt at times. Hidden with no one truly knowing her past. Veronica was the closest person she had, and had Veronica not forced her to have this night, she doubted it would ever happen.

"I need to start saving my money." Veronica laughed when Yari gave them the tour of her home.

"How many square feet is this, you plan on having a lot

of kids?" Vania dropped her bag into one of the four bedrooms.

"A little over three thousand square feet and I don't think I'll be having kids. I haven't found a trustworthy man to be putting a child inside of this." Yari rubbed her belly and disappeared only to return with wash cloths and towels to shower.

When they were done showering, they smelled food cooking.

"What the hell, didn't we order food?" Vania wasn't sure why Yari was cooking on the stove after they had spent nearly sixty dollars on dinner and snacks.

"Trust me, let her do her thing." Veronica opened a bottle of wine, poured three glasses, and shared two of them.

Vania decided to leave Yari alone as she cooked.

"You know, my family is big on large meals. My mother taught me about cooking before I became a tomboy." Vania felt at ease to speak about her family. She could see the character in both women and trusted that she could open emotionally to them.

Veronica asked to turn the heat up slightly but had already taken the liberty to increase the thermostat.

"How long have you two known each other?" Vania could recognize the freedom of friendship between the two other women. She had a bond like this with her roommate but very rarely spent time with her because of conflicting schedules.

"We met the second day I was on the force. My partner at the time had the biggest crush on Veronica and the more she turned him down, the more he tried to charm her." Yari stirred the noodles in the wok she had pulled out.

"That wasn't charm, that was some creepy shit. He would wait for me to leave and always be in the parking lot. My girl took care of that though." Veronica raised her glass to Yari.

"How did you take care of him; you didn't threaten to shoot him at 600 meters did you?" Vania was intrigued and had to ask while she refreshed everyone's wine glass.

"No, I didn't threaten to shoot him…" she paused to separate the noodles onto three separate plates.

"I did, however, make it clear that I would share a video with his wife of him having sex with prostitutes and turn the video over to our boss." Yari walked to the oven and pulled out the chicken wings she had kept warm.

They ate and talked about work and then life in general. After finishing off the second bottle of wine, the conversations became more personal. Veronica and Vania listened to Yari speak on some parts of her life growing up.

Yari had been a foster child after losing her father to a heroin addiction. Her mother died while giving birth to her younger brother. He was three months early and the complications took both her mother and brother. This was the catalyst for her father's drug use, and after no one in her extended family adopted her, she ended up in four foster homes over the course of four years. Yari told them she emancipated herself after graduating high school at the age of sixteen. She got her associate degree from a community college in a year, before being accepted into a program to get her bachelor's and master's degree.

"Why the hell did you get into law enforcement? You could be a professor or making all types of crazy money..."

"Instead of chasing crazy people?" Yari interrupted Vania's question.

"Exactly." Vania shook her head in agreement.

"Before I was emancipated, my last foster home, was the worst. One of my foster brother's was accused of stealing but it wasn't him, the father had stolen a car. The suspect was identified by the clothing they wore, more specifically an OSU jacket that everyone knew my foster brother wore all the time. Well, they came to my home and arrested him and no matter what I told them about Steve they still took him." Yari stacked their plates but Vania took them from her and rinsed them off before placing them in the dishwasher rack.

"You cook, we clean…" Vania hesitated as she opened a bag of Oreo cookies.

"I didn't think about being a cop until my cousin joined the force. We were thicker than thieves. Everything he did, I did. He boxed, so I boxed. He learned to wrestle, so I learned to wrestle. He was more of a brother compared to my other cousins. When he was killed in the line of duty, there was no way I wasn't joining the force. My grandfather did everything to stop it from happening and thus, I'm in Columbus."

The ladies moved from the dining room into another room set up with a television and only futons on the floor.

"Neither one of you better talk shit about my furniture. That's next on the list, to be honest I've only been in this room twice. Veronica picks this room to fall asleep when she stays." Yari turned on the television and a commercial for a Mixed Martial event was shown.

"Oh, shit. The fight is tonight," Vania said with genuine excitement in her voice.

"The girl from Ohio has her title fight tonight," Yari interjected. She scanned the PPV options and went to purchase the fight, but Vania stopped her.

"You said you have an Amazon Firestick, right?"

Yari shook her head yes and switched the input on the television.

"Let me show you something, and don't go calling the police on me." Vania added programs that allowed the fight to be watched for free. In fact, she opened a program that allowed for future free programming including Pay Per View options.

As the women watched the preliminaries together, they felt the bond between them had strengthened.

They fell asleep on separate futons before the main event came on.

"The b-team got through most of the visitors log on Friday and Saturday. We can take the rest." Everett was waiting on Cole when he arrived to work Monday morning. He had spent Saturday evening and all-day Sunday with his children, and after participating with them off at a school program, he found his way into the precinct. He wore a Black Lives Matter T-shirt.

"What the fuck, Clark?" A new detective that had come over to this location when the departments merged yelled out at him, interrupting the partners conversation.

"My kids are mixed—black. I have a diverse family. Say something disrespectful, and you won't be able to talk for a month when I'm done with you." He had made it clear that his job and career was to protect and serve the community with his brothers and sisters of the thin blue line, but his children and family would always come first.

"Yeah, that one's got a low IQ partner..." Cole slid his sunglasses down to stare at the detective who turned and walked away.

"I need coffee first." Cole kept walking into the break room.

Cole hadn't slept much over the weekend. He drove up to Port Huron and took Malcolm's boat out to Put-in-Bay Saturday and had returned at 5 a.m.

"I was looking over the last five names on the log in sheet and look who signed in with his government name." Everett handed Cole the sign in sheet for a Representative Stills.

"Let's bang his door first." Cole put the sheet back into Everett's desk.

Everett shuffled around in his desk drawer and found two rubber bands and put one on each wrist.

"A reminder for Mason's basketball tryouts at 6:00 pm."

"I hope he gets his skills from Robbi." Cole mustered a joke.

Everett shook his head, turned his computer off and

grabbed his car keys. Mason had gotten his athleticism from both his parents, but Robbi was the All-State point guard with her choice of Division 1 universities to attend.

"We need a drive thru when we leave. I need something stronger."

Everett bit his tongue. If Cole wasn't such a good detective, he would have a huge concern with him burning the candles at both ends. The fact of the matter was, Cole had been the best partner he had; outside of his elite military group.

Monday morning typically had an odd feel to it. Morning traffic was more congested, and people tried switching lanes only creating more gridlock. City buses hoarded two lanes to make sure they would not get trapped behind drivers unwilling to allow them to merge.

Pedestrians created even more of a log jam as they weaved in between stopped cars. The breakfast food carts were set up and manned with familiar faces and savory smells.

Cole spent the time thinking about Spade Grimes, personal bodyguard to one of the biggest criminal bosses in the Midwest. He was respected by those who earned money and power in the shadows. If he hadn't pledged his loyalty to Crusher, there was no telling how far he could move up the ranks.

"A friend told me that he would be on site to the

development downtown. Seems that the project that Representative Stills put a hold on is moving forward now.

Everett pulled next to a dump truck being loaded with debris and garbage. Empty paint cans and blue five-gallon buckets were overflowing from a garbage container. They exited the vehicle and walked directly into a group of five men talking.

"Are you guys taking reservations yet?" Cole interrupted a dark-skinned man speaking with the supervisor of the job. He stood almost six feet four inches and both detectives were familiar with his history, even though the only criminal charge on his record was disorderly conduct.

Spade Grimes had been the go-to person for Derrick Crusher for over fifteen years. Crusher had helped him out of a bind with a group out of Chicago. Since then, he remained loyal to Crusher's vision.

Spade watched them approach before responding.

"Gentlemen we aren't open for business." He had no fear in his voice, it was more of an amused tone.

"I thought this project had come to an end," Everett said straightforwardly. He looked at the last two men before they got the indication to leave.

"Look, what the fuck do y'all want. Clark you don't have to make small talk with me. Get to the point or get the hell off of private property." Spade didn't raise his voice, but his tone became cold.

"Orlando, why did you see Representative Stills on the night he was murdered?" Cole was nursing a headache and found himself being impatient. If Spade wanted to get straight to the point, Cole obliged.

Spade looked at Cole intensely. Something changed and the energy shifted.

"Orlando is what my family has permission to call me and I don't have swine as family. So, do me a favor, if you want to speak with me about anything. Get a warrant. Now please leave before I call the police." Spade regained his composure, laughed, and walked away.

Everett shook his head and exhaled.

"That wasn't the best idea calling him Orlando. You know he gets triggered by that." Everett wasn't certain Spade would've shared anything with them, but he knew once Cole made it personal all bets were off.

"Yeah, I know, but you saw the look on his face when we told him indirectly, he was a person of interest. I think the best option right now, is to track down the person who approved construction to be completed so quickly." Cole finished as he sat down in the car and finished off the remaining latte with two extra shots of espresso.

"That fight was so good." Travis had excitement in his voice as he spoke to Jack and his partner about the MMA title fight over the weekend.

"I thought her elbow was going to be permanently damaged, how the hell did she come back and win." Bryan, Jacks partner asked.

"Jiu Jitsu." Vania walked in and threw a plastic store bag onto her desk. Her khaki pants and mahogany Cleveland Browns long sleeve shirt matched her boots.

Travis nodded to acknowledge her arrival and continued speaking with the other detectives.

Vania got a text message from the facility that Alexa was being cared for.

"She woke up."

Vania's eyes widened and she felt butterflies in her stomach. Relief was her first emotion, joy followed and the smile across her face forced wetness from her eyes. She walked into the restroom to wipe her face.

"I didn't know where you vanished to." Travis was sitting at his desk when she returned.

Vania sat down and opened her store bag. She slid two energy bars to her partner and placed the rest inside her desk drawer.

"We've got a couple of leads called in to the hotline yesterday. One caller in particular says he knows who pulled the trigger and would cooperate, as long as they got the reward for helping apprehend the killer." Travis opened on of the energy health bars to eat.

"Did he leave a name too?" Vania wasn't sure that the caller was viable.

Travis stared at her for a moment. Her sarcasm was expected but for some reason it rubbed him the wrong way.

"I didn't take the damn call..." he paused because his voice had carried, and a few eyes were drawn their way.

"No, to answer your question, but we have an appointment with him at the little market on East Livingston and James at 9:45." Travis finished.

Vania played back the conversation in her head and saw how he could have been offended.

"Am I driving or you?" She didn't feel the need to respond negatively to her partner, or anyone for that matter. She thought about Alexa coming out of her coma and made plans to visit her as soon as possible.

"I'll drive and thank you." Travis saved the second energy bar to take with.

Rush hour had died down and the cars in the parking lot of the strip mall were filing in. Several mom-and-pop stores were situated between more modern establishments. A popular nail salon always seemed busy.

Travis drove to the back of the store front and parked.

"This is not what I expected for Monday morning, to be..." Vania paused as a lone male figure walked toward them.

He kept scanning around and looking over his shoulder. They had been on a higher alert level with many in the community voicing their concerns and frustrations over policing in their neighborhood. One officer had been shot at, and no suspects had been apprehended yet.

Vania and Travis unholstered their guns at the same time. Although this was a tip called into the hotline, they would not be caught off guard.

"What's up?" Travis called out through his window.

"What you mean what's up? Y'all the police or sumthin?" He kept looking around before making his final approach. His hat was pulled down across his eyebrows and his eyes barely visible.

"Yeah, we the police, one time. 5-0." Travis wasn't sure that this was the informant with that greeting but the man relaxed a little.

"I don't like none of them names or people associated

with them, but I do love greenbacks, so dig. I heard Joe Stills owed money to some people and they had him killed. If the information I provide leads to arrest and conviction, I get the 25k no questions, right?"

"Who are you?" Vania asked. She didn't like the whole set up and was skeptical. She tugged at the waist of her Cleveland Browns shirt so it would not catch her holster.

He looked through the window at her and then again at Travis.

"Deon, the dispatch hotline people have my info, and if they didn't, you wouldn't be sitting here bumping gums with me."

Travis needed the information before his partner said something.

"What's the name of the suspect?"

Deon watched a delivery truck drive down the small corridor behind the stores.

"Tobias Mack. My source says he's bragged about it and still has the murder weapon. Let me get y'all card, so I can have proof I spoke with y'all asses."

Travis reached into his center console and handed Deon his card. Vania gave him her name.

"That's cool. I don't need yours."

"You can have mine too once you tell us where to find

this Tobias Mack."

Deon laughed uncontrollably and grabbed his crotch.

"Why do you think I had you meet me here. He's the manager of the shoe store." He nodded towards the rear entrance of a store specializing in urban footwear.

"I don't need your card, just make sure I get paid." Deon stared at Vania for a second and then walked away from their vehicle, still checking his surroundings.

"Run the name through the system, we need to know who we are dealing with." Travis wasn't sure why Vania was short and snappy, but he didn't have time to let it affect the case.

He drove around to the front of the building and called the shoe store number; a voicemail came on to advise normal business hours were 12-7 and to call back during those hours.

"We have an hour and a half before they open, we can check with the lab…" Travis was interrupted by his partner.

"I need to see someone." Vania gave him the location to head. She was charged emotionally and couldn't wait to actually see the young girl whose life she saved.

"What are we going to get a warrant for?" Everett was explaining to Sheldon they had no grounds to ask a judge to sign a warrant to bring Spade in for questioning.

"We need more than a name on a piece of paper. The last time we rushed to justice, ended up costing the city a half a million-dollar payout with an apology."

Sheldon shook his head in agreement. He understood, but it was Ms. Toll's emotions that drove the conversation.

"We can't put faces to anything in the lab. We take whatever evidence and give it to you. Joseph Stills deserves justice."

Ms. Tolls looked up from her workstation to make sure Everett and Sheldon felt her frustration.

"I know your job ain't easy detectives, but neither is ours." She then went back to running tests on evidence samples from a different case.

Everett pulled Sheldon back into an office for privacy.

"Malcolm has a way of accessing company feeds, can you get into their computer system? I'd like to know what Shepherd and Zoey are keeping away from the public. Every politician has secrets and right now something simply isn't adding up."

Cole called Everett and ended the dialogue between the forensic specialist. The younger detectives had the name of a suspect who had been seen around the campaign headquarters.

"They verified that the suspect had words with both Shepherd and Ms. White. Representative Stills intervened. Vania and Travis are running down his whereabouts..." Cole's voice faded before he told Everett they had a guest.

Spade and his attorney were sitting in Captain Montgomery's office when Everett got back to their floor.

"I didn't expect this." Cole watched the captain give a fake smile and handshake to the attorney as he and his client departed.

Captain Montgomery called them into his office.

"So, we just got threatened with a lawsuit should any further harassment be levied against Spade or the property under construction. I was provided an alibi for Spade and it's pretty airtight. He was with his employer at a private event held with the mayor in attendance." Captain Montgomery received a phone call and waved them out of his office.

"I hope the b-team is having more luck than we are." Cole checked his phone for an update.

"Frances Hiller made some strong political arguments against Stills; the last election was bitter." Cole sent a text to Travis.

"It won't hurt to test the temperature of the Hiller campaign now. There's been talk already of someone being appointed until the next cycle. Let's see where Hiller stands." Cole had his head in his phone and didn't see the woman sitting at his desk.

"Hi, can we help you?" Everett spoke out first.

The long braids flowed over the woman's shoulders. Her cocoa brown skin was smooth, and her green eyes stood out.

Cole had never seen her before, so he quickly surmised this wasn't a personal visit.

She stood up and shook both detective's hands.

"I think I have some information about Representative Stills."

Everett asked her to follow him to an interview room, but she declined.

"I don't get involved in police investigations, but he didn't deserve to be killed and our community needed him. I own the beauty supply store a building down from his headquarters. I saw someone walking out of the back-parking lot when I was leaving after doing inventory. His name is Tobias Mack, a wanna be thug, acting like a businessperson."

Cole wrote down the bits of information that she shared. His phone rang.

"Yeah, yeah. Bring him in." Cole ended the call and got

the contact information from the business owner.

They thanked her for helping and watched her leave.

"The same name she just gave, is the same person Vania and Travis have tracked down. They're in the Short North watching him at happy hour. Travis ran background and it seems Tobias has an outstanding warrant from Child Support."

Everett was hesitant to think of this as a win. Something didn't feel right.

A suspect out of the blue was dropped into their lap.

"It might be a stretch for a warrant, but we need the murder weapon. I'll call the ADA's office and see what they can do." Everett sat down at his desk and made a call to facilitate a warrant for Tobias Mack and his property.

"Y'all got me down here for child support?" Tobias knew it was a false pretense.

"For starters. Where were you four days ago between 2:30-5:00 am?" Vania didn't want to play games. She dove right in.

Tobias thought about his answer and then shrugged

his shoulders.

Travis had the statement from the beauty supply shop owner.

"A few people saw you near Representative Stills HQ. You were arguing with someone earlier in the week. You came back that night to prove a point?" Travis knew from Tobias' background that he had been in the dope game most of his life. Once Representative Stills had good cops on his side, Tobias' business took a hit and the neighborhood he had been assigned lost money.

"How do you own property and multiple cars but can't take care of your child?" Vania hoped the question rubbed him the wrong way. It did.

"It's females like you who think you have all the answers. I take care of mine and don't need a crooked ass system geared toward chicks who get knocked up and then claim to be victims. But since you asked. The house they live in, I pay for that. Every doctor's visit for my child I pay for that and I have receipts. You think the money I spend on a monthly basis isn't to support my child? The mom has already filed a motion to drop it...." He paused and sat forward.

"I've done all I could do in my former lifestyle. I got into it with the campaign people because they wouldn't accept a donation from me. They took money from all types of people, but my money is no good. Kinda hypocritical don't you think? Now to answer your original question, I was in bed asleep, alone. I have cameras to verify. Now if you have any more questions outside of Franklin County Children Services, I will exercise my right to remain silent."

A tap on the double mirror was an indication for the detectives to leave him alone, for now.

Captain Montgomery was waiting on them.

"Good job, I didn't think he'd say much. A warrant was issued and executed on his home and vehicles. Keep him in interview room two." Captain Montgomery wasn't sure that Tobias Mack was involved in the death of Representative Stills, something felt... off.

Everett and Cole walked straight into interview room two and placed the handgun on the table. It was secured in an evidence bag with date, time and location marked on it.

"Felons are not supposed to have guns Tobias." Cole motioned towards the bag on the table.

Tobias had a look of surprise on his face.

"Why did we find the possible murder weapon in your

home?" Everett followed up Cole's statement.

Tobias looked even more confused.

"Man, that ain't mine. I don't know where y'all got that from, but it ain't mine." He denied the allegation.

"My forensic department is staying until they run all the tests on this weapon. They will run test after test, and if this was used in murdering Representative Stills, child support is the least of your worries," Everett added.

"Get me my lawyer. That's all you get from me."

Cole and Everett walked the gun to the forensic lab and were directed to have Ms. Tolls run the ballistics tests.

"I really don't like this feeling I've got that we are being led to this conclusion. When was the last time we got a layup? This is a layup." Everett watched Ms. Tolls pull for prints.

"Two separate sources point to Tobias, we have his server, which will have video of his home. If his alibi holds then we are right back to where we started." Cole saw Veronica working and made eye contact with her when she looked up. He cared for her, more than he had any woman in more than a decade. Since his college years, when he wasn't mature to keep the only woman, he knew he had loved. This was one of the reasons he had not dated Veronica again. He knew he could not give her what she desired. It was an honest conversation, and in the end, friendship was the only thing left on the table.

"How long before we can expect…" Everett tried asking but was cut off by Sheldon.

"Detective, would you ask Malcolm that question? The salt and pepper specialist asked his own rhetorical question.

"Right Shelly." Everett made his way out of the lab.

"I didn't mean it to be taken…" Sheldon attempted to call out, but Cole touched his elbow to indicate 'let it go'.

"I'll be working on this all-night, Cole!" Ms. Tolls called out.

"Representative Stills meant a great deal to many, including our former colleague Gene. We will find what there is to find." Sheldon shook Cole's hand before checking Veronica's progress.

Cole took one final look at Veronica and left. He wasn't sure if he was capable of exposing his emotions to anyone, if he was strong enough to be vulnerable again.

"Tobias, the gun we found is the murder weapon. Your prints are the only ones on it. We are charging you with murder in the second degree, unlawful possession of a firearm by a felon, and the list goes on. You know the drill." Cole sat across from Tobias and his lawyer.

"I will have you out on bond by the morning. You have other evidence to process, like his surveillance footage. If your department has rushed to judgement because the press and city is calling for someone's head to roll, we will pursue every option at our fingertips. I'd like a copy of the ballistic report." Tobias' lawyer finished before directing his client to remain silent.

Cole acknowledged that a report would come through the proper channels with the proper paperwork requirements.

He left Tobias to speak privately with his attorney.

Travis and Vania were standing by the whiteboard with the names assigned to each case.

"It's not over yet. Where's boss man?" Cole looked around the office space but didn't see Everett.

The younger detectives shook their heads in unison, they didn't know either.

A news alert flashed across the televisions mounted against the walls.

"Breaking news, an arrest has been made in the murder of Representative Joseph Stills. This just in and we will have more information to give you as it comes in."

"How the hell did they find out so fast?" Travis stared at the television.

Cole had no answer for his younger counterpart.

"It just doesn't feel right." Vania said while staring at the news, coming back on air with the evening news anchor.

"We have Wendy Stills addressing the recent loss of her husband."

The next live feed showed Wendy at a podium. Her nanny stood close to her with the children in strollers. Shepherd and Zoey could also be seen on camera.

"We lost a leader and voice in our community. A champion for those wanting a better life for their families and friends. Joseph always greeted everyone as family and friend." She paused as a few people let out 'amens' to support her claim.

"This is the reason I am standing here today, because his vision must shine brighter now than it ever has. I have received condolences and prayers sent for these three angels who must live without their father, but they will know him. They will know him through the good works he did for all of us, and the work we will continue in his name. It will take all of us to keep his legacy alive. It will take all of us to fight the corruption that he met head on. Our criminal justice system is not perfect. Joseph wasn't perfect, but he fought for change, and if you let me, I will continue his fight. I will be running to occupy the seat my husband left behind."

"I couldn't do it." Vania moved away from the whiteboard and television.

Everett walked back in and had an exasperated look across his face.

"Robbi is taking Mason to the hospital." He shook his head in disbelief.

"What?" Cole asked.

"He and his friends set up a bike jump ramp. It broke, he fell and is dinged up. I'm going to meet her." Everett left quickly.

The three remaining couldn't figure out what to do next. The case was closed, and their day had ended.

Malcolm walked into the office space with a huge grin on his face. He had changed his clothing and had an aura of energy as he approached.

"I just passed your boss, and I'm thinking, since the party pooper has left the building, first rounds on me."

Malcolm ushered them off and out of the building.

CHAPTER THREE
ChOICe

The picket signs were frequent on both sides of the protest. Those gathered this morning yelled at each other. The morning rush hour had settled down and traffic wasn't as congested from the drivers slowing down to look at the police presence and yellow tape.

"Every child matters!" a woman's voice shouted, and the sign she held high above her head repeated these same words. A young woman undeterred walked inside of the Health Clinic for Women.

"Her body, her choice!" A second set of voices matched the intensity of the opposing group.

The building only contained the address on it. There were no business signs to indicate what businesses were located inside of the building, but it had housed the clinic that offered abortions for the past fifteen years.

The yellow tape helped keep the groups from physical altercation, but the tension ran high in the morning hours.

"The kids haven't even been born and they're fighting for the rights of the unborn, when there are so many kids in poverty right now. Hypocrites, I bet these are the same people that used to scream "All Lives Matter" when the Black Lives Matter movement took root." Vania didn't mince her words as Travis pulled into the parking lot of the business.

"We need to move this crowd back. I don't want them yelling at me this early." Travis parked and exited the vehicle with his partner.

"Hey, Jones." Travis approached one of the uniformed officers standing watch over the body, now covered with a sheet to keep out of view of the public.

"Hey, Travis. What's up, V.A.?" He greeted the partners and gave them a preliminary account.

"From what we can see, two shots to the back and one to the head." Officer Jones pulled the sheet back to reveal the body.

"Identification?" Vania asked as she bent down to inspect the body.

"Dr. Helen Navarro. The body was found by two employees when they arrived this morning. Navarro was always first to arrive daily. They have cameras overlooking most of the building." Jones nodded in the direction of the two groups still screaming back and forth at each other, as a dead body lay in the parking lot.

"Names of employees?" Travis asked.

"Gretchen Marks and Penny Borjski."

"We will speak with them and get access to the cameras. Push them back as far as you can, but try not to escalate anything. The last thing we need is that media crew to spin this with our faces plastered across the news." Vania directed the officer who obliged.

The building was worn with minimal windows. The security guard manning the door buzzed the detectives in after they showed their badges.

"You must see all types of shit on a daily," Travis said as he held the door open for Vania.

"Every day its' something new..." He paused as he looked at a monitor that overlooked the parking lot.

"Dr. Navarro didn't deserve that. We do more than offer abortion services. Fanatics are the worst." The security guard had them sign in on the visitor log and then buzzed them into the interior portion of the office.

The waiting room was more crowded than either detective had imagined. Some mothers with newly born children breast fed, while others sat with their partners waiting to speak with someone. The atmosphere seemed surreal. A mixture of mothers with child and others seeking advice on bringing a child into the world were reflective of those on the outside, but in here, there were no arguments.

Vania walked to the receptionist window, and Travis stood behind her.

"Please fill out the form and answer all questions with an asterisk. If you have an appointment, we will verify after you return the intake form." A woman appearing to be in her early thirties slid a clipboard under the small opening under her glass enclosure. Her freshly twisted braids accented her face, by any means she was a beautiful woman.

"Detective Aquilar and White. We need to speak with whoever is currently in charge." She flashed her badge while Travis noticed the other inside cameras.

She picked up the phone and notified the person on the other end that the police wanted to speak.

The receptionist buzzed them into the inner office and back to a room where an old white man sat behind a desk staring at a pile of folders.

"Dr. Pomer, they'd like to speak with you."

"Thank you, Autumn." Dr. Pomer stood from his desk and shook both detective's hands in greeting.

"I'm sorry this has been difficult, a very difficult day." He sat back down behind his desk and exhaled.

"I can only imagine, losing a colleague; tough. How long did you know her?" Vania sat back and crossed her legs.

Dr. Pomer glanced upward to recall memory before he replied.

"Helen, I knew her for over twenty-years. The last fifteen, she and I kept this afloat." Dr. Pomer paused as someone walked by his office.

"She was passionate about what we do here, and it's not only abortions. We do family planning, birth control, annual women's exams amongst other things. She was a much better advocate than I could have ever been."

The sound of email being received came through his computer. He opened the message and sighed.

"More hate mail."

"I can only imagine the content. Did Dr. Navarro get

mail like this too?" Travis asked as Autumn knocked on his door.

"Sorry, doctor, but should I cancel any further procedures until you find a replacement?" Autumn finished by stroking one of her long braids. She was doing her best to maintain professionalism on a morning of tragedy.

"No, no, some of these clients may not get another chance to exercise their choice."

Autumn nodded her head and walked back towards the receptionist's station.

"Helen got more hate email and regular mail than I did. It never deterred her; it never stopped her fight to make sure women have the right to choose. We bulked up the security with the gate around the building and cameras. I am almost seventy years old, and in my lifetime, I have seen the true face of humanity. Like you two, I'm sure dealing with homicides."

"We have seen our fair share. We'd like to look at any hate mail she received and look at her emails that also may point to a potential suspect." Travis looked squarely at the doctor to measure his response.

"Absolutely. Anything that you need that does not breach client and patient confidentiality, Autumn will handle for you. If you need anything at all, please contact me. I have to prepare for a procedure." He stood up and motioned for the detectives to head back to see Autumn.

Vania laid her business card on his desk before Travis handed one to him.

The judge sat above the others on her bench looking out at those seated waiting to hear the verdict of Senchin Gross. Her black robe was a contrast to her fiery red hair and bloodstone necklace. Both matching her personality, she was not to be trifled with.

The defendant, found guilty, was led away by two officers and the bailiff. Those congregated in the courtroom stood in amazement after the defiant outburst of the defendant. Everett and Cole waited for the prosecutor before they walked out into the hallway.

"I forget how well you two actually look when you put on suits and get haircuts." ADA Joyce Mckinley was happy to have just won a case that was sure to boost her credentials.

"I'm handsome in overalls and sandals." Cole laughed and then thanked her for the compliment.

"A year and a day from when we busted him. His lawyers win even when he loses." Everett had counted the days down until this trial came to court. A man murdered his business partner and wife. Covered it up by burning the bodies along with the business.

"Money can buy you a lot of things, but every now and then, justice gets served. I have to speak with the loser before I get back to the office, but Thursday night, I've got box seats to Nationwide and you both will be my guests." Joyce pulled the strap of her bag over her shoulder and walked away.

"Thursday night is the father-daughter dance, so I can't make it." Everett noticed the defendant's attorney speaking with Joyce as they entered an area reserved for lawyers.

"When was the last time you danced, please don't embarrass my niece. Becca needs you to be the cool dad during these impressionable years." Cole loosened the tie around his neck as they walked through the anteroom and down the three flights of stairs to the ground level.

"Like you're the best person to get advice on kids." Everett looked at Cole with raised eyebrows.

"Do I sense weakness in your two-step?" Cole laughed loudly as he pushed the turn- style to exit the courthouse.

Everett checked his text messages and saw that Travis and Vania were leaving the site of a homicide.

"Whatever. I need to change before surprising them with lunch today, so drop me off at my place and I'll meet you at the office in a couple of hours."

Cole stopped in his tracks until Everett noticed.

"A couple of hours will be almost four o'clock. I'm without a doubt taking the rest of the day off partner. It's been ten days in a row and whatever the b-team is working on right now they can handle it, or Capt. wouldn't have given it to them."

Everett checked his watch and looked at Cole.

"Without a doubt huh?" He asked as Cole began walking toward the car.

"Unequivocally, without a doubt."

Becca was excited that her dad surprised her for lunch. He brought pizza, enough for her to share with the four friends she had eaten lunch with for the last two years of middle school. She sat with a sense of pride watching her dad interact with her friends. This had been one of the few times she had seen him dressed up. His gold badge hung from his neck and the other students kept walking past their table to be nosey.

"Mr. Clark is it scary, some of those people kill other people, don't they?" Jefferson Myles asked. He was one of

Becca's oldest friends. Robbi and Jefferson's mother had grown up together in an old area of Linden.

"Of course, it can be scary, but that's how courage is developed. When you are afraid of something, I want each of you to remember one thing. Fear is only what a person is willing to accept. "

The table of friends shook their heads like they understood what Everett had said, but as Jefferson took a second slice of pizza, he asked his second question.

"Are you afraid of anything?"

The table got quiet. Becca looked at Jefferson in disbelief.

Everett sensing the uneasiness, lightened the conversation.

"I'm afraid of not getting to your brother's on time for his lunch." He smiled and kissed Becca on the forehead and said goodbye.

He heard Jefferson trying to explain to his daughter why he had to ask so many questions. Everett smiled as he heard the young man's reply.

"If you don't ask, you don't get, and I wanted to know."

Everett had already placed the order for sub sandwiches online as he sat with Becca. He got Mason his favorite lunch: Philly cheesesteak with mushrooms and mayonnaise. He made sure that Mason would be waiting in the office to be picked up. He was taking him to a park to have lunch and watch wildlife. The love for being outdoors was rubbing off on his son.

"Daddy!" Mason exclaimed when Everett walked into the office.

"What's up, Mason! They've said you have had an excellent week, so I've got something special for lunch."

His son's eyes lit up.

"Mr. Clark he's been better than excellent. Will he be returning for the day?" The school secretary asked as she added the time to the log of their departure.

"I'll have him back on time for his first period after lunch. Thank you so much and have a gorgeous day."

He and Mason walked out of the office.

"What you get me for lunch, Daddy?" Mason asked excited.

Everett opened his son's door and watched his eyes light up seeing the sub shop bag.

Mason turned around and hugged him.

"I love you, Daddy."

"I love you more, munchkin. Let's go, so I can get you

back on time. You can eat some of the fries in the car, but wait for the sandwich." Everett closed his son's door.

Everett felt proud to be the father of two wonderful children.

"Two things, I have an unidentified print from the victim's driver side window and on the door handle. Secondly, the amount of hate mail in just one week is crazy. You should read some of this stuff." Veronica scanned through a few emails before adding them to a program Malcolm created that would group each one based on a threat level. The program worked as good as the information input and the frequency of repeated words. Once complete, it would give percentages of people most likely to escalate or act on a threat.

"We are 20 years past the 90's and we are still having a discussion on the right of a woman over her own body," Vania said over Veronica's shoulder.

"Well, that's one way of looking at it." Sheldon chimed in.

"What?" Vania asked.

"Procreation is our truest viable way for self-preservation as human beings. When we don't produce more than die... we die." Sheldon responded without any offense. Veronica looked up from the computer to stare directly at her superior in the lab.

"Why does that matter to a woman, who had an unwanted pregnancy? Or a woman raped who gets pregnant, or will die if she carries child to full term?" Veronica blurted out with no regard as to how her words came out.

"I didn't say it mattered or didn't matter, only stated a fact. These 'or' questions are circumstantial." Sheldon walked away after his point was made.

"Stoic ass." Vania waited as an analysis conclusion was being printed out.

Sheldon kept his head in the papers he carried, nearly knocking Agent Yari into a table when she entered because he was focused on work.

"So, I hear you guys are running your own investigations now. I knew you and Travis would fit like a hand in glove." Yari sat down opposite of Veronica at her lab table.

"Yeah, the Powell case wasn't so bad, but we were over our head with the triple homicide..."

"You mean the Crusher case. I want no part of that with so many moving parts. Have they finished the investigation into what led up to the shootout? Brass always covers its' ass..." she paused,

"I heard his attorney threatened the city with going public about the cases affected by Gene."

"Malcolm's been on it, reviewing every case that Gene touched. He's using consultants from other departments in Cincinnati and Atlanta." Veronica spun around her seat before excusing herself to finish a report that Sheldon needed before end of business.

"I take it that's our cue." Yari was first to leave followed by Vania.

"Hey Yari, hold up. I heard about the kid. I'm sorry you had to be the one." Vania felt a need to speak up.

Yari shook her head because she felt the same way.

"He was the first dead victim I found. Not a spec of meat on his bones, his hair was matted. It broke my heart V.A. and we have no leads on the suspect." Yari walked into the elevator and pressed her floor before doing the same for Vania.

"This is the life we've chosen," Vania said, making eye contact with Yari one last time before stepping into her office.

Travis was speaking with Bryan about who was the 'GOAT' in basketball. Travis was a Michael Jordan fan, and Bryan being from Los Angeles thought Magic or Kobe had those honors.

"MJ undefeated in the finals. He beat Magic." Travis fired at Bryan

Bryan shot back that Magic played all five positions.

"Could MJ do that?" Bryan raised his voice to make his point.

"LBJ, that boy from Northern, Ohio the Cleveland-Akron area is the 'GOAT.' He led less talented teams to the NBA finals. He is a basketball savant. A Cavs team with Delonte West and Eric Snow, come on fellas. Bron didn't have that killer instinct when he was younger, they say, but he always made the right basketball play. He's Karl Malone and Scottie Pippen rolled into one and he just got Dwight Howard a ring too." Vania added her two cents to the discussion.

Bryan looked at Travis, who then looked at his partner. Both men started laughing when Bryan countered.

"He's soft."

Those were the last two words about the subject as Captain Montgomery called Travis and V.A. into his office.

Not knowing what the impromptu meeting was about they both felt nervous as they walked into his office.

"Both of you, sit down," he said without emotion.

He pulled out two boxes and handed it to them.

"This needs to happen. The chief made this happen,

and I don't know why she did..." he paused as the young detectives stared at their new badges.

"Now dismissed, Corporals."

A full day had passed without Vania and Travis making any progress on the death of Dr. Navarro. The program Veronica used in the lab had yielded results, but as they ran down ten leads the day prior, finding the needle in the haystack was an understatement.

They were the first to arrive at the office

"Five o'clock is sooo early," Vania said as she sipped on coffee.

Travis was loading another recorded camera view from the Women's Clinic onto the screen in the media room.

After watching the hours surrounding the murder to no avail, because where Dr. Navarro parked was a blind spot; they watched the previous two weeks on accelerated speed.

"This is pointless!" Vania blurted out. She reiterated that she was not a morning person.

Travis rewound the video file and marked the

timestamp. He then loaded up another video file and scanned it until he found what he was looking for. He marked a second time stamp followed by two additional more.

"This couple shows up religiously every day, for two whole weeks." Travis enhanced the picture of the couple holding anti-abortion signs.

"But on the morning in question, they arrived shortly before we did."

Vania, with her eyes barely opened, studied the picture of the couple until she recollected.

"Who is that they are speaking with, in the OSU hoodie and hat? Can we zoom in on her, or find another camera angle?" Vania perked up slightly.

Travis pulled up other video files, but each showed nothing to help.

"Well, we do have their license plate." Travis wrote down the license plate of the minivan they drove each day.

"Let's run this, get a name and location. I'll treat for breakfast before we run up on them." Travis slid his chair away from the video monitor and walked back to his desk.

Vania walked back to the break room and poured a second cup of coffee. She added two heaps of sugar to it to get a jolt, but quickly reconsidered drinking sugar with her coffee after her first sip.

"Whoa, whoa, whoa. We don't waste the morning liquid of the gods! What's wrong with it?" Everett asked as he approached.

"Sugar, I added too much."

Everett took the mug from her hand and tasted. His eyebrows heightened and his face frowned,

"Yeah, I think you're right, but I have to tell you, if any other old head saw you wasting coffee. You'd have to supply the break room with a months' worth." Everett shook his head to make his point.

"A month supply for pouring out one cup of coffee?" Vania felt it was overstepping.

"I'm telling you so you can save money in your pocket. Anybody other than me sees you doing it..." Everett left it at that as he brewed a third pot of coffee, knowing the morning shift would be arriving by seven o'clock.

"Clark, I thought I'd beat you in this morning. Travis has his head in the computer again." Captain Montgomery walked in carrying his water reservoir for his Keurig Machine in his office.

"You know better than that Capt." Everett responded and sipped his coffee.

Vania made eye contact with the captain and acknowledged him, as she poured her coffee into the sink and rinsed her mug out.

Everett met her eyes and shook his head in a disapproving manner.

The captain squinted at the young detective and then back toward Everett who walked out of the break room with Vania on his heels.

"V.A. I've got names and an address." Travis looked up and saw that it was Everett walking toward his desk first.

"You guys are exceeding my expectations, even without heeding my advice." Everett looked at Vania and shook his head again.

"Thanks sir, I think." Travis was unsure what message was conveyed, but with the newly found information he was certain a lead had formed.

Vania slipped her mug into one of her desk drawers and yawned. She was still waking herself.

Cole walked in from the stairwell. He checked his watch as he entered their workspace.

"So, I'm the last one?" He asked seeing the team congregated.

After the good morning pleasantries were finished, Everett gave the b-team leave to follow up with the couple.

"So, are we kicking them out the nest?" Cole sat down.

Everett looked at him and shook his head

disapprovingly.

"What?" Cole asked unsure what his partner was getting at.

"What type of sun salutation was it this morning Michael?"

Cole stood from his desk and walked into the restroom. He had lipstick on his neck again.

"Yoga," Cole mumbled as he removed the lipstick with a wet paper towel. When he returned the chief of police was walking with Captain Montgomery towards Everett, who had his back to them.

"Clark, I saw White and Aguilar are outworking you and Playboy Pete." Captain Montgomery nodded as Cole approached.

The chief smirked and put her hand on Captain Montgomery's shoulder.

"His jokes have always been stale. I'd like to take you both to breakfast, there's something I'd like to discuss, a new idea that David and I think makes sense. My driver is pulling the van around, I'll meet you all downstairs." She looked at Captain Montgomery before they walked away leaving Cole and Everett to catch up.

"What the hell? It's not even eight a.m. yet and no Crimson Cup." Cole was big on surprises when they came from women; but being blindsided not so much.

"Who knows, but I'm sure it can't be worse than my therapy session this afternoon." Everett scooted his chair away from his desk and walked down the stairwell.

The sign on the door read "Choose Life, LLC."

Travis pushed the glass door open and stepped into a bland office space with pictures of babies and families spread over the ecru walls. Christian Music was playing quietly over the speakers. In each corner were small lamps situated on small glass tables.

"I feel like we just walked into the nineties." Vania shrugged her shoulders as Travis looked back at her.

"Good morning, how may I help you?" The receptionist greeted them with joy in her voice.

"Well good morning to ya, it's such a great day isn't it?" Vania matched her perkiness.

"It sure is, every day is a good day to praise The Lord. Are you guys here for a consultation?" she asked.

Travis showed his badge to her.

"God is good all the time. I'm Detective White and my partner Detective Aguilar. We'd like to speak with Erin and

Landon Murphy."

The receptionist seemed surprised and called back to notify them of the detectives arrival.

She buzzed them back into the office and walked them into a conference room where anti-abortion signs were being made by a group of people.

"Diane make that exclamation point in red and twice as large, remember this is your voice, so make it loud."

"Detectives, it was only a matter of time before you showed up here. I told my wife as soon as the body was identified that we'd get a visit." Landon Murphy approached them and waved his wife away from the group making signs.

They looked vastly different than they had the previous day at the Women's Clinic.

"Hoodies and hats yesterday. Khaki and Loafers today. I can see it in your eyes detective." Erin Murphy approached and allowed her husband to kiss her cheek.

"What's that Mrs. Murphy?" Vania was curious to what she meant.

"That we are frauds. Portray something in the public and then run a business like this. A fisherman doesn't wear waders unless he's fishing. You don't wear your badge all the time, do you?" Mrs. Murphy walked into their office with the others in tow.

"Water, soda?" she offered as she pulled a 20oz. Mountain Dew bottle from a miniature refrigerator.

Vania asked for a Pepsi and Travis glanced at her.

"What? I'm thirsty." Vania opened the bottle and took a gulp. Her facial expression changed as the first bit went down.

"Before you ask us, we can tell you that we had nothing to do with that murder. We value life." Mr. Murphy sat on the corner of the desk.

"Is your group typically the one that shows up first to protest?" Travis asked as everyone else drank beverages.

"If you're not first, you're last." Erin gave her husband a look.

"Yes, if you're not first, you're last. I know honey."

Vania wasn't going to let their exchange pass without prodding.

"Is that your catch phrase or tagline?" She sat forward in her chair and placed her Pepsi on a coaster.

"It's something our predecessor drove into us. We needed to be at the place of protest before they opened, before any workers arrived. It was constant pressure, or the perception of it that grew our cause," Mrs. Murphy answered.

"How long has the location off Morse Rd. been

targeted by your organization?"

Travis asked as the office phone buzzed.

"Hold all calls..." Mrs. Murphy was cut off by the person on the other end.

"Janiece, hold on, honey. You're talking too fast. Okay, okay, we're on the way." She hung up and looked at her husband.

"The kids have been trying to call you. They're stuck on the highway. Why haven't you answered your cell phone?" She opened a desk drawer and retrieved her purse.

"One thing before you go. Why weren't you guys 'first' yesterday at the clinic?" Vania needed that answer before ruling them on or off the suspect list.

"Because my wonderful husband flooded our basement the night before last and we had a company come out first thing in the morning yesterday. Now, please excuse us as we go assist our children."

"Name of the company, so we can verify please." Vania decided to be kind; they were not what she expected.

"Dry restoration."

Mrs. Murphy escorted the young detectives back to the front of the office, exiting the way they came in.

"You and your team of sleuths have been busy the last few months. On behalf of most of the citizens of Columbus, I say thank you." Dr. Simmons greeted Everett and closed the office door behind. This psychologist had been the only one he had ever seen. Initially ordered to see him after killing two murder suspects in the line of duty, Everett kept seeing him after those sessions ended.

Initially Everett thought it was a waste of time. He had been able to compartmentalize aspects of his life after serving two tours during wartime. Dr. Simmons, however, became a valuable tool for him to vent about everything other than work.

"How are the kids? The last time I saw you Mason was getting a belt promotion. How's Becca?" Dr. Simmons sat down opposite Everett in a white leather chair.

Everett, on the matching loveseat, brought Dr. Simmons up to speed, but the Doctor could sense something else troubling his client.

"It must be an interesting topic if it has you second guessing yourself on whether or not you want to share it with me."

"My team barely escaped a shootout, my department, along with the forensic department, has been compromised, two of my team is going undercover, and

Robbi's dating again, a woman."

Dr. Simmons jotted down a few things in his notepad.

"So, seventy-five percent of your rant is job related and the rest is about your ex-wife? Often the last thing out of my patient's mouth is what is heaviest. How does it make you feel that Robbi is dating again?" Dr. Simmons cut through the façade Everett was trying to maintain. It had always been what weighed the most on his heart, his family. Everett had a firm belief that his military tours and police work was the ultimate sacrifice in protecting his family, and Dr. Simmons helped him see the truth of the matter.

"Isn't it, obvious doc? I don't know how I feel about it. I haven't had time to process…"

"No, you haven't made time." Dr. Simmons interjected to make sure Everett spoke honestly.

"I haven't made time to process. The kids are good, our relationship has never been better. I attend their school events and they stay every night that I don't have to work the next day. I am taking them to protest this weekend." Everett shook his head.

"The children are going to be ok because their parents are ok. Sure, there will be an adjustment with new people being brought into their lives, but we still aren't speaking about how you are dealing with Robbi, dating a woman." Dr. Simmons wasn't going to let Everett off the hook that easy. He put his notepad down, sat back in his chair with his legs crossed and waited for Everett to get to the truth of the matter.

"I don't care if it's a woman or a man. I still love her with all my heart, but I am still the same person. I think making sure the city is safe is the best protection I can give to all of them."

Dr. Simmons chuckled.

"What?" Everett asked.

Dr. Simmons picked his ink pen up and wrote something in his notepad.

"Is that what you really believe? Most of the time you are straight forward and honest, except when it comes to dealing with familial matters. If making the city safe is the best protection, why are you still enlisted with the military?" Dr. Simmons felt his client needed to be pushed because he was close to a breakthrough.

Everett looked perplexed. Of all the questions he thought he would be asked; this was not one of them.

He took longer to answer. Everett reflected on his enlistment after getting his bachelor's degree. When his father was killed in the line of duty, he thought the best way to honor his father was to follow in his footsteps.

"Hmph, good question. Honestly, my CO is waiting an answer on another tour. I'd be Stateside, an instructor for those moving into special forces. It's a lot of responsibility, maybe more than I want to take on." Everett paused. Dr. Simmons facial expression told him that he wasn't being completely open.

"I'm not going to re-enlist." Everett finished.

Dr. Simmons picked his notepad up and jotted additional information.

"You know I've always hated when you've done that. That little notepad of yours is not my friend." Everett smirked.

Dr. Simmons looked down at his notepad before he turned it so Everett could read his last entry.

'Finally, being honest.'

Everett wasn't sure he understood what it meant.

"You're finally being honest about your feelings. You wanted to walk in your father's footsteps, which you have done and excelled. You wanted to protect this country; you've done that. But what matters to you the most, frightens you. It makes you hesitant to express vulnerability." Dr. Simmons paused and closed his notepad.

"I want you to think about something and ask yourself this; do you throw yourself into dangerous situations with the military or your line of work as a defensive mechanism, so you don't have to deal with your fear of being vulnerable?"

Everett disagreed vehemently at first, but as he thought about it, he understood the true answer wouldn't come to him so quickly.

"This day has not started off the way I expected at all. I'm going to think about the answer before I respond." He checked his watch and scheduled his next appointment for one month out.

"Detective, not to place too much on you but I see things vastly different than most. You are great at whatever you decide to put your energy into, and you lead with ferocity. Use these two traits for your personal life, what's the worst thing that could happen?" Dr. Simmons stood from his chair and shook Everett's hand.

Everett turned his head as he walked out of his Psychologist's office.

"You're a hard man to please."

The Murphy's alibi had panned out, and with no other leads, Vania and Travis got back to reading through Dr. Navarro's email. Repeated threats and series of profane words were the common thread amongst the content. Some stood out more than others, and those were flagged for further investigation.

"Maybe we should look into her personal life a little deeper. The first thing we did was jump to a conclusion that it was related to the clinic." Travis was getting tired of reading the assorted emails.

"I'm open for anything at this point. I have her address in German Village." Vania wrote the house address down and ran a quick map quest on her work computer.

"Why are people smiling at us?" Travis asked as he looked at a few of the faces of other detectives.

"Who knows and who cares." Vania followed Travis out of the office and down the stairwell.

The day was slowly passing, early evening was setting in and the intensity of the sun was dying down. The amber hues faded, but with a few hours left before dusk, the young detectives drove the back streets to avoid the tail end of rush hour.

"I thought about moving to German Village when I first moved down from Cleveland, but I didn't want to spend over fifteen hundred dollars on a place with limited space."

Vania stared at some of the older brick homes they passed.

"It's a nice neighborhood, but for fifteen-hundred dollars a month, you should be an owner."

Travis appreciated the upkeep of the neighborhood. Working professionals who didn't have adequate time to fully appreciate all the 'things' they accumulated.

"I pay a little over a grand for my place, and it's twice the square footage. I had to do a lot of the work, but it saved me money and gave me a new skill set," Travis finished as he pulled into the driveway of the recently departed Dr. Helen Navarro.

Two other vehicles were parked in her driveway.

The detectives exited their vehicle and walked into her home unannounced. Their presence had been overlooked, until someone saw them as they pulled boxes into the front of the home.

"Can I help you?" a woman asked as she made eye contact.

"Detectives Aguilar and White with the Columbus Police Department. Who are you guys with?" Vania nodded in the direction of another man and woman who were pulling other items into the front room.

"Cynthia Navarro, Helen's sister." She removed her work gloves. There was a thickness in the air, but neither Travis nor Vania understood why. The sunlight flowed through the oval shaped front windows. Small particles of dust could be seen as it brightened the whole space.

"We are sorry for your loss. We are running down

every lead we come across." Travis was interrupted by Cynthia.

"Oh, so, now you want to run down every lead, protection isn't worth a damn when my sister ends up gunned down. Y'all didn't want to help when she was still breathing, why the hell would you care now!" She stomped her foot onto the dark hardwood floor.

Cynthia was approached by the other woman who asked her to finish helping the man still hauling things into the front room. She hesitated before pulling her jeans up at the waist.

"You have to excuse my sister. I'm Melinda. Yesterday was hard on us, and Cynthia has a right to be angry. Being denied protection orders against repeat offenders who skirted the law when they threatened her was infuriating, so you can see now, when you two show up, that it's a little too late."

Melinda took a breath realizing she was growing impatient. The man reappeared in the front room with more items in his hands.

"Mel, I have to be back to close this deal in less than an hour. I'll bring a few guys and we can finish up tonight. Cynthia, answer anything they ask, these civil servants are working on behalf of Helen." He disappeared into a back room and pulled one additional box to the front room before speaking with the detectives.

"Helen was the strongest and most intelligent person I've ever known, and I deal with Hedge Fund guys and businesses on the Fortune 500, people who think the world revolves around them. Helen could've done anything in life, and she chose to help those in need..."

"She put her life in jeopardy for damn near fifteen years helping people and it ended up getting her killed. We don't need you trying to manage us Brandon." Cynthia approached the group again.

"We are here to find the assailant who took the life of your sister. We read hundreds of emails she received at work, you mentioned failed restraining orders." Travis needed to break through the family squabble and get everyone back on track.

"Yeah, the last one she filed was less than a month ago, but they threw it out because not all the conditions of being harassed and stalked had been met. Have the conditions been met yet, now that she's dead, this is fucking ridiculous." Cynthia could not control her emotions.

"I'd be pissed at whoever put my family member in harm, and I'd do everything I could to get justice for them. My partner and I are here right now seeking justice. What can you or any of you tell us that gets us closer to justice for Helen?" Travis understood he needed to calm emotions and put everyone on the same goal - justice for Helen.

Mel took Cynthia's hand and led them all to sit as the brother Brandon left the home to attend to business matters.

"Besides the threats from her occupation, was there anyone else that could have wanted to harm her? Was she dating, involved with anyone romantically?" Vania asked as the tension faded.

Cynthia was first to respond.

"Helen didn't have time to date. She had a mission to save the world." Cynthia began to form tears in her eyes. Mel grabbed her hand for support.

"Actually, she reconnected with a man she dated about eight years ago," Mel added.

The look on Cynthia's face was that of surprise.

"Patrick?" Cynthia asked her sister.

"Yeah, Patrick," she answered.

"Why would she date that piece of shit. He was having an affair with her and it nearly broke her when he didn't divorce his wife. Why would she let him back in her life? Why wouldn't you stop her Mel?" Cynthia pulled her hand away from her sister and walked into the kitchen area. She stood at the dual sink and turned the faucet on to rinse her hands off.

"Who could've stopped her from doing what she

wanted, you couldn't, and I couldn't. Don't blame me or anybody else. She was her own woman and you know that!" Mel began crying and Cynthia walked back to the couch with paper towels in her hand.

"I know, I'm sorry. I'm just pissed and sad all at once." A heavy burdened was felt as she exhaled.

Vania hesitated before diving back into questioning. She understood some of the emotions being shared, as she reflected to packing her cousin's belongings after he had been killed in the line of duty in Cleveland years ago.

"You mentioned Patrick. What can you tell us about him?" Vania sat forward to show she was intent on what they had to say.

"Patrick Albion, advocate for women's rights. The Champion of Choice," Mel said.

"Piece of shit adulterer," Cynthia interjected.

"Yeah, piece of shit. He strung Helen along for three years as he was always getting papers signed for the divorce, but nothing happened. We lost the light from my sister for over a year after that breakup," Mel finished.

"Is there any reason to believe that Peter would want Helen harmed?" Travis asked.

"No, he treated her with love and thought the world of her. His lack of respect is what caused her to doubt herself." Cynthia reflected.

"How can we find Patrick Albion, do either of you have his contact information?" Travis listened intently as Vania asked questions. He felt it much more productive to have her do the interview; woman to women.

Mel excused herself as she retrieved her purse from the dining room table. She searched her contact list before writing down Peter's cell phone and office number. She gave them the address and name of his firm.

Cynthia looked at Mel with a strange look.

"Don't look at me like that. When Hell's Bells told me about Peter coming back into her life, I needed to make sure he understood that if he played with her emotions again, it would be the last time he ever did."

Mel looked at her sister and smiled before pouring out tears.

"I know this is hard on your entire family and saying anything seems inadequate. We will do everything we can to bring Helen's murderer to justice." Travis paused knowing the next bit of information may not sit well with either sister.

"We have to ask you all not to remove any of the items you've boxed up until further notice."

Vania waited for a rebuttal and she would make sure they both understood the importance of being patient, but both sisters understood.

"Here's our cards, if you have anything else to add or that you find out that may help us, please contact us." Travis stood up first and shook their hands.

Vania matched the sister's motion and stood up as they did.

"We are truly sorry for your loss." She touched them tandemly on the shoulders, making eye contact with both before she walked out behind her partner.

Travis saw her eyes were beginning to form tears as they strapped their seatbelts on in the car.

He had learned his partner over the course of almost a year and knew this was a moment she needed to herself. He could only believe that his partner was reliving the moment she lost her cousin.

As he backed out of the driveway and put the car in drive, Vania input the next address into the GPS and stared out the window. She wiped any remaining wetness from her face.

"Thank you, T."

"I got you V.A., I always got you partner."

"Do you have an appointment with Dr. Albion?" One of the two front staff receptionists asked Vania and Travis as they walked off the elevator. Her red glasses were a stark contrast to her frosted color hair. Her counterpart wore white glasses, with her hair colored jet black.

The waiting area was quaint, yet vibrant. Two large fish tanks carried an assortment of colorful salt-water species. A mother held onto a baby and pointed to the fish as she spoke with her child. She glanced back momentarily, making eye contact with Travis.

"No, not necessarily but is he in?" Vania watched as the receptionists looked at each other before she was answered.

"He is, but without an appointment he is unavailable. We can get you scheduled for four months out. We understand it's not ideal, but we can refer you for another qualified physician." She adjusted her red glasses and raised her eyebrows, waiting for a reply.

Vania ascertained that the two had held conversations like this in the past. The second receptionist answered an incoming phone call.

"Five months won't due, we're kinda impatient." Vania flashed her badge.

The receptionist hesitated as she thought of what to do next. She picked up her phone and dialed an extension to advise that the police were in the lobby for Dr. Albion;

shortly after a short woman wearing a houndstooth dress with purple blouse and matching shoes came out to greet Travis and Vania.

"Dr. Kirsten Glass."

They followed her to an interior portion, seemingly, Dr. Albion's personal office space.

"Detectives come in. We have refreshments at your disposal." She pointed to an all-glass refrigerator stocked with iced coffee and various sodas.

"Please have a seat. He will be with you shortly."

She departed from a different door than they had entered.

The office had two different views of downtown Columbus. The furniture was high quality as was the desk. The various plaques of achievement frequented the spaces between the windows. Pictures of Dr. Albion with State Senators, both past and present, mixed in with all the other accolades.

Kirsten walked back in followed by Dr. Albion.

"Detectives, I can only assume that you have questions for me about Helen." He walked to the refrigerator and retrieved two energy drinks.

"Ask me anything. We reconnected about six months ago, after meeting by chance at a mutual conference. We were learning..." he paused to correct himself.

"She was learning if she could forgive me for some things I did in the past." He opened one can and drank down the entire contents.

Kirsten excused herself.

"Thank you, Dr. Glass. If you can take my next appointment and offer my apologies."

She shook her head affirmatively and closed the door behind.

"From our understanding, you failed to live up to her expectation of ending your marriage to start a life with her." Travis decided a straight-forward approach was best.

"All true." Dr. Albion agreed with Travis. He stood up and retrieved a bag of pretzels from a large wired basket containing snacks.

"It was one of the worst decisions I could've made. Helen and I were perfect for each other but my ambitions for power, enough power to truly make a difference overshadowed everything else." He sat back down.

"Did you kill Helen Navarro?" Vania was following Travis' lead.

"What? No, I didn't kill Helen. I wanted her back in my life, for good and forever." He ate a few pretzels before drinking his second energy drink.

"What about your wife? Don't you think she'd have something to say about that?" Vania had become irritated with this answer and didn't care if her tone sounded offensive.

"My wife, ex-wife and I divorced three years ago. It had nothing to do with Helen. She and I had not spoken in years at that point. Now please, ask me some questions that will help find her killer. My time is valuable, and this is a courtesy." Dr. Albion's tone also shifted.

"Where were you yesterday morning between the hours of 5:30 am and 7:00 am.?" Travis jumped back into the line of questioning. They needed to find answers and Travis could sense the energy building in the room.

Dr. Albion ate a few more pretzels while staring at Vania who returned her own.

"Flying back from Chicago after meeting with the Mayor of Chicago about new initiatives." He opened his computer and clicked a few times before the printer activated. Dr. Albion pushed his chair back and walked to the device.

"Here's my flight schedule, and the hotel I stayed in. Let me walk you out." His demeanor had changed after Vania pressed him with attitude.

Vania stood up and was handed the print outs. She walked out of the office first.

"My apologies, this case has a lot of moving parts. Is there anyone who might hold a grudge that you can think of that would take it to this level?" Travis asked one final question.

"In her line of work, the threats always came. I would think someone who was holding onto a grudge. She was a careful woman." His voice cracked and he swallowed hard. He was becoming emotional.

"Dr., thank you for your time. We are sorry for your loss." Travis walked out of the back office and into the lobby where Vania was waiting by one of the fish tanks.

"My cousin used to love fish; he didn't have community tanks like this. Black Piranhas in one tank and African Cichlids in another. They fought for survival. He had the nerve to buy a Caiman..." She paused and laughed loudly.

"Until my grandfather whooped him for doing something illegal." She walked to the elevator and pressed the down button. Travis could relate and genuinely chuckled with her, even they were not any closer to finding Helen Navarro's killer.

As they drove away from the interview, both of their cell phones received a text message for them to come to the office immediately.

When Travis and Vania walked into the office, Cole was waiting on them.

"V.A., you and I are going to finish working this case together. Travis, you're needed in the captain's office."

Travis felt nervous and the emotion flashed on his face.

"What the hell, Cole?" Vania asked because the words had been stuck in Travis' throat.

"Oh, no, no, he's not in trouble. He's going on a special assignment. I'll fill you in along the way, but Travis get your ass in there."

Vania bumped her partner in the shoulder as a sign of solidarity before they went separate ways.

Travis walked into Captain Montgomery's office, and surprise was plastered on his face.

The chief was present along with Everett, Yari, and Captain Montgomery.

"White, you're going under cover with Yari." The captain told Travis to have a seat.

"Here's the file on your cover and the target." Everett handed Travis several files.

The chief excused herself from the office.

Travis read the file of the target first.

"Don't worry. He's going to be okay. The HT Squad is closing in on the mastermind behind the case we broke open earlier in the year. I don't know how long he will be in the field with Yari, but I trust the two of them can handle whatever comes their way. Now where are you with the Navarro case?" Cole wanted to keep Vania focused and needed a rundown on the interviews they had conducted thus far.

She gave Cole an overview of each step from the clinic to Dr. Albion.

"In fact, let me check his alibi. I was going to look through the footage again from this morning. We have two weeks' worth of video. Dr. Navarro's siblings thought Albion was no good for her, but my gut feeling says he's not the one." Vania sat down at the desk to make confirmation calls.

"I'll get started on some of the footage. Six eyes are better than four." He disappeared.

Vania was speaking with the airline when Travis walked out of Captain Montgomery's office followed by Yari.

"This is going to be interesting." Travis shook his head

like he didn't know what to expect. He pulled out his notepad and dropped it on Vania's desk.

"Come on honey, or do you wanna be called 'bae'?" Yari held the biggest grin on her face.

"We get to play house. I cook; he cleans..." she paused and smirked.

"V.A. don't worry, I'll bring your partner back in one piece. "

Everett exited last.

"Where's Cole?"

"Media room," Vania answered.

Vania watched him walk away in the opposite direction of her partner and Yari, when the voice on the other end of the phone returned to verify the first portion of Dr. Albion's alibi.

"Thank you so much." Vania stared around the office as she thought through the events of the day.

Familiar faces were stuck in paperwork or staring at computer screens. A few desks were occupied with detectives taking statements from witnesses of various crimes. She reached for Travis' notepad and opened it and began reading his scribbled mess.

"Somebody with a grudge." Stuck out in her mind, but so far no one believed Dr. Navarro had enemies except those picketing her place of business. Vania hated concluding; she knew she would have to take her time in the media room watching footage again.

"V.A., this is the couple you interviewed?" Cole pointed to the Murphy's.

She confirmed.

"Who is this, the person they are speaking with in the hoodie?"

"Uhm, we...I don't know." She knew the best answer was the truthful one.

"Well, we need to speak with them. Tomorrow morning our first stop is Dr. Albion, he seems like the only enigma in her life over the past year. Maybe someone was getting at him, through her." Cole kept sorting through footage.

Vania had seen Everett leave. It was his time to spend with his military unit.

"I don't know how he does it," Vania said out loud.

"What?" Cole's focus had intently been on the computer monitor.

"Oh, nothing. I mean Everett and all the training stuff." Vania expected more of an exchange but decided to leave it alone after Cole simply replied.

"Yeah."

Vania returned to her desk to call the hotel that Dr. Albion had stayed, making confirmation that he had been a guest.

She felt tired suddenly, and hungry. Looking at the time on her computer screen, she realized that she hadn't eaten since breakfast and it was fifteen minutes after seven.

"V.A. take off and get some rest. I'll catch myself up and look at all the notes. Don't come in here before eight. I need you fresh." Cole walked out of the office disappearing down the stairs.

Vania didn't second guess her superior and closed her computer.

When she arrived at home, her roommate had left her dinner in the refrigerator. She showered after eating and passed out until her alarm rang the next morning.

Vania rode in the passenger seat as Cole expressed some of the ideas he had regarding the case. She was amazed to see him work firsthand; Vania understood she still had a lot to learn about being a detective.

They were buzzed in again and met by Autumn.

"Who is typically last to leave in the evening?" Cole had taken charge in asking the second round of questions at the women's clinic.

Autumn was answering the questions but seemed to be flirting with Cole in the same instance.

"It's usually one of the physicians. We have a cleaning crew come in overnight." She reached for one of her braids and played with it.

"What about security? Are they twenty-four hours?" Vania was curious seeing a different security officer when they arrived.

"They're supposed to be, and they are supposed to walk the perimeter of our lot once every four hours, but that doesn't happen. They sit and watch the monitors unless they want to take a smoke break." Autumn excused herself as Dr. Pomer walked into his office.

"Ahh, detective, I see you have a new partner today. Any break in the case? Things have been hectic the last few days. I never knew how much Helen handled on a day to day basis. The staff has taken her death hard; trauma presents itself in so many ways." He sat down after removing his white coat.

"Dr. Pomer, I noticed you received a lot of funding from the Albion Group. How's that relationship been?" Cole asked.

"They carried us for several years, provided legal advice when necessary. Julie and Patrick Albion have championed our cause for decades." Dr. Pomer pointed to a picture of him alongside Helen, Julie, and Patrick in several photographs hanging on his wall.

"Julie and Patrick are divorced; she kept his name?" Vania said to no one in particular; she was thinking out loud.

"Yeah, that surprised me too. They were a power couple, I guess the name still has weight. Why not use it I say." Dr. Pomer seemed to get lost in thought.

"Julie is really the force behind the business, but Patrick's connections grew the business. I heard the Albion Group is pushing a multi-state initiative that will help fund clinics that have had legislation passed to derail our efforts."

Autumn knocked on his door for a scheduled procedure which cut the interview short. Vania bid Dr. Pomer, farewell as Autumn asked Cole for a business card and if it was ok to call him if she had anything further that she could help with.

Vania walked out the building first, slowing down so Cole could catch up to her.

"I didn't think they were right," Vania said as he unlocked the doors to their car.

"Right about what?" Cole dropped the key fob accidentally. When he stood back up, Vania was waiting to answer his question.

"You're a whore." She laughed as she said the words.

"Whatever." Cole smirked, rolled his eyes and got into the car to drive to Dr. Albion's office.

"Sorry, we are taking up more time today. I know you are a busy, man. We confirmed your alibi, but I wanted to ask about the Albion Group. It's kept separate from your practice" Cole made himself appear humble to cater to the superiority complex Dr. Albion had. Cole also noticed the photos on the wall with various politicians and celebrities. He saw an identical photo to the one in Dr. Pomer's office.

"Absolutely separate. One is my career and the other my legacy," he answered, before offering the detectives refreshments again. He removed energy drinks as he had the day prior, along with a bag of pretzels.

Cole grabbed a soda and a bag of pretzels to join him.

"I know divorces can be sloppy, how were your career or legacy affected by it?" Cole asked easily.

Vania was reminded to one of her grandfather's

sayings, 'it's easier to catch bees with honey than vinegar.' She realized she could have made more progress the previous day had she taken the same approach.

"I can tell you one thing, the lawyers made out hand over foot between Julie and I fighting over the things we loved the most. In the end, we fired all the attorneys except two of them. We agreed on a settlement that made us both content with what we received, while allowing us to maintain our active roles in the Albion Group." He opened a can and drank down half.

"What was Julie and Helen's relationship, did they get along?"

Vania decided to let Cole ask all the questions.

Dr. Albion sat quietly for a brief moment before he answered.

"Strangely enough, Julie was Helen's biggest advocate. There were years I wanted to pull a portion of the funding, but Julie fought against it. She won of course." He drank the rest of the energy drink and opened his bag of pretzels.

"The affair, did your ex know about it?" Cole asked his next question as he chewed pretzels.

"No, she never did. I almost left Julie for Helen. Helen always wanted to tell Julie because she felt guilty. It would've destroyed all the good that was built. In the end we decided it was a secret we needed to keep."

Cole thanked him for his time and asked where to discard the empty items he consumed.

Cole led Vania out of the office and commented on the fish tanks.

"Sometimes predators act like prey in order to eat." He left it at that knowing his point had been made as she agreed with him and added one final observation.

"We should speak with Julie."

"It's a shame, I saw it on the news earlier. She did good work for women who needed choice." Julie Albion sat on her back patio with the detectives overlooking a portion of the Olentangy River. Her two German Shepherds ran freely throughout the yard.

"Your ex-husband says that it was you, the driving force behind the Albion group. Have things changed much since the divorce became final years ago?" Cole asked a different line of questions.

Vania kept her eyes on the dogs as they chased a rabbit that appeared from the hedges separating the neighbor's property. It ran behind a shed and that's when

Vania noticed a red sweatshirt like the one in the video, she had watched of the morning Dr. Navarro had been shot.

"Not as much as I would like, but we are on the verge of something big. Patrick finalized a proposal in Chicago that will help so many that need it."

Everyone's attention was drawn to the dogs trying to get in between the space of the hedges and tool shed.

"Smoky and Craig, come here!" Julie called out and immediately they stopped and came to sit in front of her on the porch.

"When was the last time you talked to or had seen Helen?" Vania asked the question out of the blue, having a gut feeling.

Julie held her hand out for her dogs to approach and lick her hand. She then waved them to go back out to the yard and play.

"God, I haven't seen Julie in almost six months. Their funding is good for another three years." She finished before excusing herself to get ready for a video conference with the Governor's office in California.

Vania nodded towards the shed and made sure that Cole saw the sweatshirt before they left.

"I know. We need a warrant."

"How can we get her prints?" It was the first question our of Vania's mouth as they pulled out of her driveway onto Dublin Rd.

"Let's confirm that she was the one on video that morning. Whoever it was spoke with some people before they left the scene, have we interviewed anyone she may have had communication with?" Cole was relying on Vania and Travis' initial movement with the case.

"We spoke to a couple who looks like ordinary protestors, per se. But they run a multimillion-dollar business, and they definitely don't look like they did on video." Vania looked through Travis' notepad to look at the notes he jotted down on their previous visit and shared them with Cole.

"They are our next stop. You have a copy of the clinic's video footage on your laptop?" Cole asked Vania.

"Uh, I don't think on this laptop, but I do have it on USB." Vania was learning tidbits from Cole and she stored them to use at a later date.

"Good always keep a tether to information you can use readily when needed. These Murphy's, you checked their alibi with Travis. Why was that interview cut short?"

"Their children had broken down on the interstate and

needed rescue." Vania and Travis had not dived deeper into the children of the Murphy's, aged and sexes.

"Remember one answer leads to more questions until you are satisfied. Do we know if the children were at the protest like their parents?" Cole asked additional question so his younger partner on the case would be better prepared in the future.

As they pulled into the parking lot of Choose Life LLC, Cole noticed one of the vehicles that had been parked at the scene of the murder. He walked by it to look inside.

"I hate minivans. Minivans equate to having children, and that's a non-starter for me," Cole mumbled but loud enough for Vania to hear.

"Well, they are saving the world," Vania said with sarcasm.

"Judgmental a bit today, V.A.? Is something bothering we should talk about?" Cole reached out to touch Vania's hand.

"Our personal experiences help us most of the time, but sometimes they can cloud judgment. Let's not do that today."

Cole walked into the business.

When the receptionist saw Cole, she smiled but that was quickly erased as Vania walked in behind him.

"Detective, more questions?" The receptionist did not wait to call back for either owner.

She buzzed them in, and Vania led the way back to the office area of the Murphy's.

"Did we run your other partner off yesterday?" Erin met Vania's eyes as they all took seats.

"He's got a new assignment, so she brought me today." Cole interjected to get control of the conversation.

"We checked your alibi and are pleased to rule you and your husband out. My associate indicated that you have children. Do they participate in your business, were they protesting over the past two weeks?" Cole wanted to keep her off balance until he could ask the one pertinent question he needed answered.

Erin shifted uncomfortably and crossed her arms.

"My children are passionate about our cause, and they understand the power we create for Pro-Life supporters. My children are in school daily, like most children who want a better life." She finished with an edge in her voice.

"I was just discussing with Detective Aguilar that I'm not the parenting type. I love children and watching them grow from a distance." Cole quickly jumped back in to lighten the mood.

"We have footage of you and your husband speaking with someone the morning Dr. Navarro was killed." Cole paused as Vania pulled out her USB and loaded it on her laptop computer.

"Can you tell me who this is?" Cole pointed to the Murphy's and the person in the red hoodie and boots.

Erin looked at the computer screen and then at Cole.

"Big Brother is everywhere. I don't know who the woman was, but she seemed supportive of our cause..." Erin paused.

"She seemed familiar but honestly people often think I'm somebody else." Erin sat back with a little less tension in her body.

"Erin, if you saw her again. Would you be able to identify her, do you think your husband could?" Vania asked the one question that held on her lips.

"I don't know about him, he's a smart man but can be absent minded. But yeah, yeah I'm sure I'd be able to."

Cole thanked her for her time and led Vania out of Choose Life.

"I can't be sure until we get back, but I believe there was correspondence from the Albion Group to Dr. Navarro in the emails we looked at. Are you hungry?" Cole had not eaten yet and his stomach was grumbling.

"If you're buying boss man, I can eat." Vania was hungrier than she let on.

"I'll treat, but I'm not buying." He turned into the parking lot of Club Ekans and saw Rachel's car, a black Audi A8.

Vania had never been at this location before, and as she walked up the small incline of stairs, she was surprised to see a room half-full of business professionals having lunch.

"Cole." Rachel saw Cole as she returned from the stock room.

"Hey, Rach. This is..." Cole was interrupted

"V.A., detective Vania Aguilar. Cole thinks he keeps his job separate but as much as he talks about his team, I feel like I know you already." Rachel hugged Vania and returned to the bar area.

"What are you eating V.A.? Do you need a menu?" Rachel slid a lunch menu across the bar.

"Thank you." Vania sat with her head in the menu while Rachel and Cole talked.

She gathered Rachel had a roommate or girlfriend that enjoyed Cole's company.

Whatever that means. Vania thought before ordering the fish and chips.

"Good choice, for bar food." Rachel walked the order back to the kitchen herself to get a rush on it.

"She's pretty," Vania said as she moved her chair to listen to a man speaking at the microphone.

"Our appreciation to you is unparalleled. Sonja will be handing out envelopes with bonuses for each, and every one of you. Some will be more than others, but remember hard work pays off, and smart work pays even more. Make sure you show your appreciation for the servers, as they have done a wonderful job taking care of us." The man motioned for a woman to pass out the bonuses.

"Money makes money." Vania mentioned it as she wondered how much the bonuses were.

"After we eat, we need to find a viable option to get a warrant for Julie's home." Cole's phone rang and he excused himself.

Rachel returned and gave directions to a bartender to make sure everything was stocked for happy hour later.

"V.A., is it ok to call you that?" Rachel asked.

"Sure, if I can call you Rach." Vania winked at Rachel to let her know she was just joking.

"This is the first time I've met anyone from his life. He's grown on me and my partner." Rachel was interrupted by a bar back changing kegs.

"So, needless to say this is a pleasant surprise." Rachel had to move again to allow the bar back more room.

"Your food should be almost ready, give me a sec." She walked away, leaving Vania to decipher Rachel had an open relationship, that included Cole.

Cole sat back down at the bar, as Rachel returned with their lunch.

"I had Sheldon look through professional databases that require fingerprinting for those with fiduciary responsibilities. Guess whose prints were on file and matched the unknown prints from Helen's vehicle." Cole shook his head in a positive manner because the case was closer to being solved.

"So, we got our warrant?" Vania asked as she poured ketchup on her plate.

Cole had taken a bite into his double cheeseburger and couldn't respond verbally, so he shook his head.

"Such an appetite on this one." Rachel added while placing napkins on the bar for their use."

"Rach, do you have malt vinegar and hot sauce?" Vania dipped one of her fries into the ketchup.

Rachel nodded and walked back to the kitchen to return with both items requested.

"I usually hand out Tabasco sauce, but for you, you get my personal stash. I have a meeting in ten minutes with Mr. Bonuses up there. Vania it's been my pleasure, you should come back for one of our event nights, if you have an open mind." Rachel walked to their side of the bar and shook Vania's hand and allowed Cole to kiss her on the cheek.

They quickly ate in silence. Cole got up to leave and Vania was uncertain about payment.

"It's comped." Cole acknowledged.

Vania walked back to the seat and placed a ten-dollar tip under her plate and then walked down the stairs to exit the building.

"We got a foreign set of prints off two of the driver side windows the morning Dr. Navarro was murdered. From your own admission you advised us you had not seen her in six months or so. How do you explain your prints at the murder scene?" Vania was leading the questioning.

Cole wanted to help sharpen her closing skillset.

Julie sat quietly. She had no answer that would make sense.

"The red sweatshirt that we saw as your dogs chased the rabbit around your shed, is identical to the one on video. It's being tested now for gunshot residue. What was so bad that you had to kill her?" Vania sat back as the video played of the Murphy's speaking with the woman. Erin Murphy had already identified her through a photo collage.

Julie Albion sat quiet and listened.

"Helen was successful, and your organization was a large part of that success. You supported her for over fifteen years, why would you..."

Julie interrupted Vania

"Speculate all you want, ask anything you want, show me anything you want, but until my Attorney arrives, I plead the fifth."

"So be it Mrs. Albion." Cole stood up from his chair

"Ms. Albion. I am not married." She corrected him.

"That's right, you are divorced. That must've been tough, nearly losing your identity. How did it make you feel knowing he had an affair while you were married?" Vania jumped back in.

"He said the biggest mistake of his life was not divorcing you earlier, but you were the ticket for his legacy. I guess you both got something out of it. It had to infuriate you to know that he loved someone else and kept you around for business purposes only. I guess love can be fickle..." Vania kept edging her on and the redness of Julie's skin was an indication that she was getting overwhelmed.

"Adulterers, cheaters all the same to me, but the women always get…"

"We always get the short end of the stick. We can build a man a dynasty, but his little head seems to make decisions that can destroy what's built. He wasn't going to build anything without me, and Helen. Helen was a liar, she was a…." Her statement got shortened as her attorney walked in to complete the interview.

"I'm sure she asked for her attorney, now if you two excuse us; my client and I have to speak." Jonathan Rember walked in. A highly qualified defense attorney, that had deep connections and deep pockets.

Cole and Vania walked into the hallway.

Jack was hauling in a murder suspect. From the looks of the scuff marks on the knees of his pants and his shirt being ripped, there had been an altercation.

"Assaulting an officer was the last thing you wanted to do." Jack's partner followed with a secondary suspect in tow.

Cole walked into the break room and sat down on one of the loveseats.

"We've done our job and it's up to the DA's office to get the rest done." Cole nodded at Captain Montgomery who walked in carrying his Keurig Reservoir to fill with water.

"The ADA is speaking with Rember. Without a confession, they'll have their work cut out, but you two gave them more than enough." The captain departed with water in his container.

"You and Travis will be good detectives eventually. Hold your emotions though V.A., it clouds judgment and causes more harm than not." Cole walked back just as Julie Albion was being led to fingerprinting.

"You'll be out before the end of business Julie." Jonathan Rember gave his client hope before pulling his cell phone out to get his client out on bond as quickly as he could.

Cole sat down at his desk and checked his cell phone for messages.

"What the hell is this?" Vania asked loudly enough to gain his attention.

Cole looked across her desk and saw coupons for coffee.

"Did you waste the beverage of the morning gods?" Cole shook his head and raised his eyebrows.

"I poured one cup of coffee out that I put too much sugar in, but it was only one cup." Vania sat back in disbelief.

Captain Montgomery walked out of his office and placed another coupon on her desk.

"I need Keurig Pods."

He walked back into his office.

Vania stared at Cole and then the coupons on her desk again.

CHAPTER FOUR

STILL WATERS RUN DEEP

Still Waters Run DEEP

The condo was a massive upgrade from either of their homes. A three-bedroom space, with a basement and upper area, it contained all the modern amenities people of wealth enjoyed. For the past two weeks Yari and Travis had been laying the groundwork to be introduced to their target. Posing as a married couple, associates of Gary Pokinski, who had become an informant to keep himself out of jail. His underlings had been sentenced in a way it kept Gary's name clean.

"I made some eggs and potatoes. I left them in the microwave for you." Travis looked up from his computer as Yari walked into the kitchen.

"We have a meeting with Spencer Snow at seven o'clock. Gary will make the introduction; I'll speak more on the artwork and you the financials. Malcolm built this portfolio and if it holds like our aliases, we will be fine." Travis closed the laptop computer and walked to his room to rest his eyes before taking a shower and getting dressed.

There had been a few learning curves along the way for the two of them. Travis was a neat freak and Yari, not so much. Travis fell asleep on the couch with the television on, which was a pet peeve of hers. They had separate bathrooms which suited them perfectly. It had been a learning curve for both Yari and Travis as holding hands or showing other signs of intimacy in public had been foreign. It became more natural over the course of the first three days. Luckily, besides the occasional kiss on the cheek, no other signs had been necessary.

Travis did appreciate Yari's motherly nature, and she thought his attention to detail around the condo was a pleasant surprise. The first week undercover was to make their faces known around circles that Spencer Snow frequented. Bumping elbows with his associates, who would undoubtedly research Langdon and Sylvia Carr.

Wealthy by inheritance, they invested in winning companies. As art philanthropists, they donated more than twenty-thousand dollars to separate galleries and expensed a five-hundred-dollar lunch with an art director who had been friends with Spencer Snow since childhood. Now the Carr's had been invited to a private showing at Spencer's home an hour outside of the city.

Yari did a forty-minute workout on the elliptical in the basement. A full rack of free weights and bench also frequented the lower level. The two had worked out daily, but Yari did cardio twice a day since they had gone undercover. Her alarm went off on her iWatch to end her workout. A call from her commanding officer came shortly after.

"We have it covered sir, yeah today at seven. Copy that." Yari was ending a check-in call with her supervisor as Travis walked back from his room dressed in a fine black suit, shaved, and neatly groomed. His shoulder holster hung loosely.

"Should we be strapped?" She was unsure it was a good idea for a first meeting with the accountant of Derrick Crusher. She finished the last bit of food on her plate before rinsing it off. Her Garfield the cat leggings were the only item besides her hair dryer and toiletries she had brought from her home, everything else was at the expense of the 187epartent.

"I think Spencer would think it strange if we weren't.

I'm sure his background will list us as being intelligently cautious. Showing up to his home without protection, with predators like him, will make us seem foolish." Travis shook his head in a disapproving manner noticing that Yari had left her glass and napkin on the dining room table. He placed her glass in the sink and tossed the napkin in the trash.

He called Vania but it went straight to voicemail.

Yari reemerged from the back bedroom wearing a black Puff-Sleeved Peplum Blazer pant suit that fit her curves nearly perfectly.

"Fix your leg holster." Travis pointed as her pant leg bulged.

Yari straightened her pants and slid her ankle boots on.

"The car should be here in ten minutes. I already wrapped Spencer's gift. Today of all the days, we gotta be on our A-game. Do you have everything?" Yari stood up and walked to one of the three mirrors in the front room to check her make-up.

"I know honey." Travis winked at her and used the restroom one last time.

"Baby, the car is here. I'll be outside." Yari yelled as Gary rang their doorbell.

Travis realized the performance had begun and got into character.

"I'm coming, you, sexy beast."

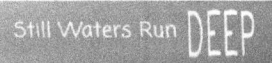

"Clark, I just heard you're headed into true civilian life." A brunette with her hair pulled back, approached Everett in uniform. Her designation, Chief Warrant Officer 2 was shown by her insignia on the right collar with a bursting bomb.

"Gunny, I have to walk away while I can." Everett headed to meet her. His disposition was better as the conversation ensued.

"I've thought about it myself, but what would I do in civilian life. Date and boss people around, I can do one of those things on base. Maybe both, if I had a clandestine partner, but you're leaving." She met Everett's eyes.

Everett had been attracted to Keiko Marshall in more ways than one. She got the absolute best from her soldiers and commanded respect from her peers. He had never looked at her purely sexually, although she was a physical specimen.

"Oh, you're too good for Civi's?" Everett laughed very loudly.

The guard manning the entry gates stared through his booth at the two before three loud horns were heard drawing their attention to a group of vehicles returning to base.

Two VLRA 2 trucks led the vehicles and were followed by Humvee's. A few soldiers saluted the pair as they entered the lot of the base.

"I have a month left before my duty ends. Grab some drinks and grub before I'm completely off limits to you." Everett decided he needed to start dating again, and if there was mutual interest, he'd like to know more about her.

"First Sergeant, I said a clandestine partnership, not a proverbial hookup. Friday evening you will pick me up, take me to dinner and I'll determine what will be for dessert." She bit her bottom lip and excused herself.

Everett watched her walk away and found himself still staring as she glanced back and smiled.

"Everett Clark, be careful when you shoot above your pay grade." A deep husky voice brought Everett's attention back to his surroundings.

"Black, yo, what's good brother?"

A small group of three soldiers walked across the lot in muddied fatigues and boots. These were friends Everett had made over the years through tests of fire and survival.

"Diamond J and Frost." Everett greeted them all.

"Keiko Marshall walking you to your car, you must have pissed her off." Frost patted Everett on his back. He received his name from his frost-colored hair and Diamond J, named from tattoos on his body.

"I just had a talk with the CO, I've decided to head into civilian life and before any of you get any ideas that you can talk me out of it..."

"Brother you have to do what your heart tells you to do. If I'm being honest with you all, the thought has crossed my mind, but I've got less than three years left on my enlistment." Black spoke up. He removed his sunglasses to wipe the sweat from his face with a bandana in his back pocket.

"How long?" Diamond J opened his canteen after asking the question.

"Thirty days or so before I have to sign my papers of separation." Everett felt a shift. He understood that the relationships he had made decades ago would be changing. The common thread was being loosened, he hoped that it would never be undone completely. He had shared life and death moments with these men.

"This weekend we will make the sixty-minute drive to Columbus, Wright-Patterson AB has worn me out." Diamond J emptied his canteen over his head to cool off.

"We need to clean and get prepared for Overview." Black motioned to those he arrived with it was time to go.

"Clark, you will always be part of this thing..." Black paused, they all looked around the Air Force base.

"Brothers always." Frost interjected and they all repeated it.

They each hugged Everett before walking deeper into the base.

Everett wasn't sure what the next part of his life would bring him. He watched members of different branches of service moving slowly after being drilled for five days straight with minimum sleep.

His phone buzzed with a text message.

"Friday at 1600." It was a number he didn't recognize but with the straightforward directive, followed by an address and the initial KM, Everett saved the number before responding.

"Copy that."

He got into his car and took a final look at the base before pulling through the guard station.

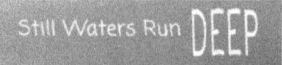

The drive wasn't as long as expected. Yari and Travis had gone over the things to expect from Spencer Snow when they arrived for the 'special art showing.'

Gary was being forthcoming with everything. His quality of life depended on it. Many of the homes they passed were newly constructed, while others faded with the changing of time. What once was a proud farming community, was now a small collection of farmers holding on to a memory of yesterday, with a farmer's market seen off road as cars filled the lot.

"These are prideful people and Spencer had to purchase roughly twenty percent of the land in this county to make his point.

"What point was that?" Travis asked.

"That money talks."

Gary's voice faded as the driver pulled into a long dirt driveway. As the home came into focus, it was much more than either officer expected.

A large ranch style home was surrounded with open spaces and fenced in areas for the multiple horses grazing. A large pond took up more than an acre of the front yard. The large glass windows on both sides of the entrance seemed like after-market upgrades.

The closer they got to the house, they noticed a tennis court, and to its side a swimming pool with men and women splashing about.

"Are they..." Yari stared through the window.

"Naked, yes. If this surprises you, then maybe you

aren't ready. These people are fun and games but make no mistake, they are predators." Gary's door was opened by the driver and they exited the vehicle.

Two large men guarded the entrance. They did not hide the fact that they were armed, and their mere size was intimidating.

"GP, he's expecting you all." One of the two men shook Gary's hand, before allowing them all to pass, and the other opened the entrance to the home.

People were scattered throughout the front room, being served cocktails and hors d'oeuvres. The scantily dressed servers were available for purchase. Gary took a glass of champagne from one server's tray.

"Drink something and loosen up." Gary motioned to a bar area where top shelf liquor was being served.

Yari reached out and took Travis by the hand and walked to the bar.

"I'll have Ketel One and tonic, and my husband will try the Cornerstone Rye, neat." Yari took charge and positioned herself more intimately with Travis.

"I know you like Whiskey but try it." She pulled back with a smile on her face.

Travis felt the various eyes moving in their direction, so he kissed her on her neck.

"Langdon, Sylvia let me show you more of the artwork you came to see." A woman approached with Gary in tow.

"I'm Lisa and my job is to make a lasting impression on you." She shook their hands and led them into another portion of the home. They walked into a den area and there were naked men and women stationed between each piece of artwork.

"These are our most recent acquisitions. Everything you see tonight is for sale, please don't be shy, take a closer look." Lisa watched them as Travis led Yari by the hand to look closer. They approached and then walked around both naked men and women.

"These are great bodies of work but really not our interest, we went through a phase like this, but we tend to appreciate more modern-day styles." Yari held onto Travis' hand and followed Lisa to a different room.

Active flirtation was initiated as soon as they entered the second room. Lisa walked to a well-endowed man and grabbed his crotch.

"I love all expressions, don't you?" she paused to check her iWatch message.

"We have different pieces for every art lover. Gary will show you around. I need to address a guest who has overstepped." Lisa walked out of the room with an armed guard bringing up her rear.

"Overstepping, is a kind way of saying someone disrespected Spencer. It's best if we worry about what's right in front of our face." Gary left the two and began to appreciate two women who had been touching each other as enticement.

"When in Rome." Yari walked the room.

Travis followed her with his eyes. His senses were overwhelmed. The so called 'pieces' of art were absolutely interactive, but he knew this was a forum for buying and selling services.

Yari moved closer to a woman, standing by herself and Travis joined her side.

"Honey, now this piece is exquisite, don't you think? The lines and curves, the strength of the silhouette." Yari noticed more guests staring at them so she took Travis' hand and moved it across the woman's body, being careful not to touch her androgynous zones.

"Don't have so much fun." Travis whispered into Yari's ears and then sipped on his Rye.

Yari slipped her hand from Travis and whispered into the woman's ear.

"You are valuable."

"We have more art to appreciate, you can bid on any piece and at the appropriate time it will be accepted or not. But follow me." Gary pulled the two undercover officers to other portions of the room.

Lisa joined them and had their drinks refreshed.

"Your donations to our art galleries were pleasant surprises. We know your organizations' charitable gifts have helped many others, and we appreciate new friendships. If our background information is correct, I think we may have a few unique pieces that may be more delicate in nature."

Lisa motioned them to follow her to a lower level of the home.

A woman dressed like an agent from the movie *Men in Black* was stationed outside the entrance.

"This is Langdon and Sylvia."

The woman scanned them with metal detectors and found their weapons.

"Please leave them with Maisie, they will be returned prior to leaving." Lisa asked politely but there was no room to deny her request.

"Thank you." Lisa acknowledged before Maisie opened the door to allow them entry.

Travis felt sick to his stomach as his eyes fell onto what appeared to be groups engaged in pre-orgy type activities with very young people.

"We have special viewing rooms you can take

advantage of, or watching is also acceptable..." She paused to stare at Gary.

"...with approval." Lisa removed herself from the group to speak with a set of men who flagged her down.

"This is sickening," Yari said as she smiled at a few eyes staring them up and down.

Eyes shifted and the presence of someone else was felt.

Travis saw Spencer Snow walking the lower level in a white robe and slippers. He carried two bottles of Dom Perignon, one in each hand. Behind him three more servers carrying trays, each with four bottles of the high-priced champagne.

"Sylvia and Langdon, thank you so much for coming to my mid-month mixer. How have you appreciated the different eras and styles so far?" He handed Travis a bottle of Champagne.

"We will have time to talk later, but as you can see, I have a few needy guests. Please enjoy everything." He rubbed Travis shoulder and ran his hand down his back.

Sensory overload was taking place for both undercover officers, but in order to get access to Derrick Crusher's financials, this was the route that had to be walked.

Roughly thirty-minutes had passed, feeling that an adequate length of time, they departed the lower level, donating a nearly full bottle of Dom P. to a couple selecting their choice in 'art.'

When they exited, Maisie returned their guns to them.

Had they guessed correctly; she ran the serial numbers for ownership. Malcolm had taken the liberty to register them in the alias names.

When they returned to the main portion of the event, they sat at a table and were brought menus of items available to them.

Travis ordered Prime Rib with Garlic Mashed potatoes, while Yari had them bring her Parmesan Risotto with Roasted Shrimp and Capers, but the truth of the matter neither one had an appetite after being bombarded with graphic images.

Gary returned from the lower level and sat down with them. His suit jacket was wrinkled, and he had lipstick on his neck.

"We didn't bring you to engage in your filthy activities with minors. The Feds can revoke your deal for any violation we mention." Yari was upset but she kept a smile on her face as she spoke to him

Gary waved a server down and asked for whiskey on the rocks.

"No one here is underage. Each one of them you saw downstairs are of legal age, barely, but legal." Gary motioned to Yari's plate of food and ate a shrimp from it.

"We've been her almost three hours and from the looks of it, the liquor and everything else being passed around, I'm sure this night is moving into a space that we can't partake. So, we need to be leaving." Yari slid her plate to Gary who kept eating her remains.

"What about Spencer?" Gary asked.

Lisa was speaking with other guests and Spencer had not returned from the lower level.

"Let's say our goodbyes. We leave them with a bit of uncertainty, if we depart now." Yari finished and Travis agreed.

Travis stood up and grabbed Yari's hand. They walked towards Lisa who was just finishing a conversation with two women who exuded wealth while Gary went and retrieved the driver.

"Sylvia, you and your husband have enjoyed our gallery fully, I hope."

"It has been a pleasant surprise to see that others have the same type of appreciation of art that we do." Travis spoke up as Yari turned her head to stare at Travis with adoration.

"It is true. Will you offer our gratitude to Spencer for the invite, unfortunately our night has to be called short? We have a proposal we need to finalize before sending it over to legal to make sure all the Ts are crossed and the I's dotted. We would love to have dialogue with Spencer on how to divest more of our money..." Yari hesitated as Travis squeezed her hand.

"To keep more of our money." Travis interjected.

"Finishing each other's sentences that's just adorable. I will schedule a sit down with Mr. Snow. Many people seek his attention and knowledge to detail." Lisa was flagged down by another guest, so she thanked them again for coming and walked away.

Gary was standing by the front door and indicated the car was ready, but Yari pulled Travis back to the bar.

"A double of Everetton with an OJ chaser, and a double Ketel One with two limes." She watched the bartender pour healthy shots.

"I'm a little buzzed already." Travis spoke up.

Yari ignored him and placed his whiskey in front of him.

"We just spent an evening in a brothel, I need this and I'm not drinking alone." Yari held her glass up to toast.

"To many more healthy years of being married." She said it loud enough for those in the immediate space to hear.

They took the shots and chased them down

respectively.

'You know the custom of the bar is to chase drinks with a kiss." The bartender smiled at them as he wiped down rock's glasses.

"Is that right? Well, we will have to take a..." Travis tried to speak but Yari stepped closer into his space and kissed him.

Travis instinctively kissed her back to maintain their cover.

"Cheers. Saluda. Slainte." The bartender smiled as they walked towards the exit.

They held hands but didn't speak. Even though they were maintaining cover, the kiss had left an impression on both.

When the car dropped them back off at their condo, they went to their separate bedrooms and slept off the intoxication.

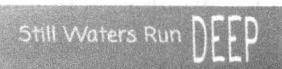

Still Waters Run DEEP

"Everett is taking the next couple of days off, it's the first true vacation days he's used in over three years." Cole poured syrup over his waffles before passing it to Vania.

Malcolm had requested their presence over food, and

IHOP was the choice made, although it was nearly four o'clock.

"He deserves the time..." Malcolm took a quick sip of coffee and handed Cole a folder with the Yari and Travis information.

"These are their credentials for your sister to add them to the guest list. Make sure it's not tied back to her directly. With your sister using her married name there should be an added level of security, but this should be the icing on the cake."

Cole scanned the file and handed it to Vania.

"They've lasted this long under cover and with the invitation for the end of the month jamboree we almost have Spencer on the hook. I can only imagine some of the things they saw at the special event last week." Cole shook his head up and down. The other two at the table weren't sure if it was in reference to the food he just swallowed, or the progress Travis and Yari were making.

"My IT guy created social media pages that are solid for the previous eight years with photos, check-ins, and various mentions on other media pages. He's a damn wizard honestly..."

"That says a lot coming from you." Vania closed the file and interjected.

"It's true though, a year ago I met him at a conference

I was a keynote speaker. He challenged some of my findings and it intrigued me. I built a position for him into the next budget but those asshats from the mayor's office are still making sure their presence is known." Malcolm mixed his hash browns with his over medium eggs.

"They're all corrupt. The commissioner, mayor and lord knows who else. If we can get Spencer Snow in our pocket, you and your IT guy can get a clean look at Crusher's financials and it could change everything." Cole asked for a refill of coffee. His phone vibrated across the tabletop. A call from San Diego, California was flashing on the screen of his cell phone.

"Telemarketers are relentless." He thanked the server for the refill and ignored the call

"Let's hope Yari and T can bring this home. The good guys need a win." Vania excused herself to use the restroom. A server with a tray full of food, was nearly tripped by two children not being paid attention to by their parents.

"Thank you." The server was grateful that Vania blocked her from taking the extra step which would have resulted in a terrible accident.

When she returned to the table, Malcolm had already left.

"Thank Malcolm later, he picked up the tab." Cole stood up and followed Vania out of the restaurant.

"Hey, do we have time to check on Travis' mom before we head back into the office? I told him I would a few times per week." Vania thought it wise, since they would be traveling past his mother's neighborhood to get to their next appointment.

Cole responded by nodding his head affirmatively as they got into their car.

Vania texted Travis' mother to see if she needed anything to be picked up, since it was difficult getting around with her car being in the shop.

"No but thank you Vania." The return text came back.

It was a fifteen-minute drive from the restaurant to her home. When they pulled up, Travis' nephews were outside racing other kids in the neighborhood.

"All of y'all are slow." Cole bolstered when he stepped out of the car.

They group of kids laughed and a voice called out to Cole.

"White men can't run."

Cole looked at Vania who smiled.

"You mean white men can't jump." Cole corrected the juveniles about the title of an old movie.

"That either." Another voice called out as the nephews separated from the group to greet the detectives.

"Hey guys, everything is good?" Vania gave them each a hug. They had grown closer since the ordeal of unlawful entry a few months back.

"Hey Aunt V.A., yeah we alright. Grandma be tripping a little more everyday about Unc. He's okay, right?"

Vania looked at Cole before answering.

"You know he's alright, and if he wasn't, I wouldn't be here. Let me check in with your grams and if y'all still out here when we come back, I may just have to show you why I hold a few track records." Vania pushed one of the nephews playfully and caught up to Cole who was speaking with Travis' mother outside.

"Mama White, I may have to embarrass your grandsons today." Vania hugged her before the three sat down on the small front patio.

"They need it honey. Thank you for taking them to karate..." Mama White laughed as she corrected herself before Vania could.

"Jiu Jitsu."

"Sounds like your son is correcting you." Vania laughed along with her.

"We can't tell you more, but Travis is doing ok. Hopefully the assignment is nearly over." Cole wanted to reassure her that her son was not left unattended.

"He's a strong man, I know he will be ok." Mama White tried to say the words with certainty, but she wasn't.

"Auntie, are you going to race us?" One of the nephews approached with sweat pouring down his face.

Vania looked over his shoulder and saw that a larger group had formed.

"A few of them boys are fast." Travis' mother rocked forward and back in her chair.

"I'm not going to take it easy on any of you," Vania said goodbye to Mama Burton and Cole followed suit.

"Is Woody Harrelson racing too?" They all laughed, including Vania.

"See, I was trying to be nice, but yeah I'm racing and afterwards I'll be the one laughing," Cole said as both he and Vania locked their weapons in the vehicle.

"Now hold on, we gotta stretch a little bit." Vania was leaning over to stretch her limbs.

"V.A., don't let these kids beat you or you'll never hear the end of it." Cole walked towards the mock starting line.

The crowd started getting loud and excited.

Travis' nephews were the youngest to take the line. Others seemed to be older teens.

Mama White watched from her porch, as did some

other parents who heard the rumbling of the group.

"It's ten dollars on the line and bragging rights." She yelled from her porch.

The crowd split, some stayed near the starting line and others ran to positions roughly seventy- yards to the end.

They took the line to get started, only to have to wait for a few cars to pass, and after one false start because Cole jumped, they took the line again.

The crowd got silent as a teenage girl gave them the countdown again.

"On your mark, get set, go!"

Vania slipped and the others got off to a good start. She caught the nephews at about ten yards. She kept her form and relaxed. Tension would only slow here turnover. At twenty-five yards she had caught up to the group with Cole and two of the other boys.

She could feel her speed as she accelerated. With a little over twenty yards to go, she caught up to Cole.

When the group crossed the line, no one could say who the clear-cut winner was.

Cole was winded.

"She would've beat all of you if she didn't slip." Mama White called out before she disappeared back into her home.

The nephews were amazed at how fast Vania was.

"You're the fastest girl we know." They hugged her goodbye.

"I thought you were going to be dusting the road." Vania told Cole as they placed their guns back into their holsters.

"All that food." Cole kept a straight face as he strapped his seat belt on.

"Don't ever let me do that again." He finished as they drove away.

Still Waters Run DEEP

Chicago O'Hare airport was bustling with energy as they walked to retrieve their luggage. An impromptu trip to add substance to their organization would surely add another building block to Spencer's trust as new clients.

Mandy had sent a car for them and set them up in a suite at the Waldorf Astoria on the company account.

The receptionist checked them in and gave them a quick layout of the surrounding area.

Yari made sure that transportation would be made available if required.

"Absolutely Mrs. Carr, you have a driver on call. We only ask to give us fifteen minutes to make sure you have no wait time." She pointed toward the elevators used to access the guest suites.

When they entered the room, they stood in awe.

A large window overlooking the city spread across half of the living room space. Purple accents contrasted against the printed pillows on the sofa and loveseat. An electric fireplace sat squarely under a mantle carved out in the corner of the room and situated above it a fifty-two-inch flat screen television.

Travis walked further into the suite and noticed a small enclosed area behind glass which contained a small office.

"Travis." Yari called out.

He walked into the bedroom with Yari looking in the bathroom.

"That's so dope." Travis eyes opened wide.

The bathroom had both shower and bathtub. The bathtub was situated close to the small patio accessed only through the bedroom. The view was astounding.

"Maybe we should do this undercover thing more often." Travis took one more look around the bathroom and walked back into the bedroom.

"I take it I have the couch." Travis slid his suitcase into

one of the closets and sat down at the dining room table.

"Let's check the city out before it gets too dark. Tomorrow we may not get time with our schedule full." Yari had returned to the front room after freshening up and changing into jeans.

"Yeah that's cool, Chicago has some great history. Do you like jazz?" Travis asked.

"I like music, as long as it's good." Yari walked back into the bathroom to check her makeup a second time.

"I've always wanted to sit in at The Kennedy Mill Jazz Club; if we get time, I'd like to..."

Yari interrupted him.

"Tomorrow we work, tonight the department is paying for our honeymoon Mr. Carr." She winked at him.

Travis shook his head and grabbed a small jacket before they left to make their mark in the windy city.

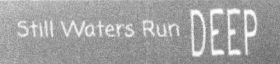

"About the mid-1800's is when this place took shape. It was originally a church and people tied their horses to the posts. Can you imagine hearing trains during sermon or Sunday school?" Everett was having a better time with Keiko than he thought possible. The conversation was fluid, they could share similar experiences of the military and relished that the other understood.

The restaurant did have an old church aesthetic. The soaring ceilings and stained-glass windows accented the upscale French themed eatery.

"I thought a refectory was a dining hall or eating room in a monastery or convent." Keiko took a sip of her red wine while looking at the massive amount of varying wood.

The dimly lit space had a unique ambiance. The wood floor contrasted nicely against the rustic accents throughout. Candles frequented each table and areas separated for larger groups, or those wanting more intimacy.

"Clark, I had no idea what to expect. Most men that I allow my time, get it all wrong. They spend more time speaking about their accomplishments until they learn I'm in the military. Then they challenge my ability as a woman to lead men, followed by apologies when they figure out that there's no chance they will get into my pants or bed."

Everett burst out laughing, nearly spitting his wine out.

"I have no problem taking orders from you." He said it in terms of serving in the military, but Keiko took it to mean something else.

"That's cute Clark. You really haven't done this in a

while." She touched his hand and made eye contact.

"When I divorced the only part of my life that kept me from falling apart was the military. I had a few one-night stands." she paused seeing Everett not fully understanding.

"Do you think men are only capable of one-nighters? That somehow, I have forgone my vows of chastity. Let me let you in on a little secret. Women want sex as much, if not more than men. We typically take quality over quantity, but when you gotta have it." She smirked at him.

The candlelight balanced the mood. The flickering of the flame reflected her alabaster complexion. Her shoulders, although strong were feminine and exuded sensuality.

Her black Bandage Strappy Dress exposed her cleavage and portion of her breasts. The design piece included a choker type fastening extending from just above her bellybutton to her neck. Her arms were exposed but accented by a sheer pattern that matched the trim nearest her cleavage. Her two-and-a-half-inch Bow Detail Print Heels brought personality to the sexy ensemble.

Everett wore deep colored blue jeans with a black dress shirt, accompanied with a black blazer and matching wingtip shoes.

"Gunny..." Everett paused and corrected himself.

"Keiko, I can't remember the last time I felt comfortable with a woman since...well you know. If you can handle a little more of my time, I'd like to take you somewhere else." Everett poured the rest of the wine into her glass and for the next hour they talked about their lives as kids growing up. Everett paid for the check and unexpectedly kissed her passionately as he opened her door to the car.

"That was nice," Keiko said as they pulled away from the kiss. She ran her hand down his cheek and got in the car.

"You probably want to change those heels. I told you I have a father-daughter dance coming up and I need practice." Everett pulled up to bar that had musical performances each night that ranged from great local bands to a few headliners.

The interior had an authentic old feel to it, like the decades held firm and only the people had changed over the years.

A band was playing more recent dance tunes and TI's 'You Can Have Whatever You Like' was in full swing.

Keiko pulled Everett to the small dance area and found a space.

Everett moved in unison with her. The light in her green eyes relayed that she was having a wonderful time with him. She pulled on her hairpiece and her hair fell to her shoulders. Frayed and full, her hair kept pace with her body movement. Now seductive and sensual, other people glanced their way.

Everett felt free. He felt no worries and he attributed it to the bottle of wine they shared, but even more so to a woman he admired and now greatly desired.

Keiko turned her back to him and kept dancing. Her back muscles shown with each twist and roll of her body. She reached back and grabbed Everett's hips to pull him closer while slowly thrusting her hips back into him.

"Turn up!" A woman approached the microphone as the band went quiet. The eyes of everyone looked at the platform and then the horns began playing the intro to J. Coles 'Middle Child.'

Keiko shifted into Everett and pressed her body into his.

Everett grabbed her waist and they danced into the night, intermittently taking shots of liquor, until the band played their last set.

"You made me feel like a woman for the first time in years Clark." Keiko looked through her small handbag to pay the tab but had forgotten the establishment kept her card.

"We want to cash out. Marshall is the name," Keiko advised the bartender.

"You guys make a cute couple," Two women said as they also waited to cash out.

"Thanks, she's actually my boss, kinda." Everett was drunk and feeling safe with Keiko.

The women laughed not knowing if there was truth to his statement.

"It's true, inappropriate business relationships. You gotta try it," Keiko added.

All four were caught in an awkward silence before the bartender laughed as he brought back their copies to sign.

"That seems to be a common theme during closing."

All four people laughed.

"I don't think I can drive Kiki." Everett had been given permission to call her by her nickname after their second shot.

"Well, I can't either, hold on." She pulled out her cell phone and ordered a driving service.

"Jonesy, you guys were beasts tonight. Give me a few minutes and I'll get you guys paid out." The bartender walked away from the band leader and moved to other patrons needing to close their tabs.

"Ten minutes and our uber will be here." Keiko checked her cell phone again and Everett excused himself to use the restroom.

Keiko was speaking with the two women at the bar when he returned.

"They bought us shots." She pointed to healthy pours of a concoction in shot glasses.

"What is it?" Everett stood behind Keiko with his body pressed into hers, he kissed her on the back of her neck.

"Does it matter at this hour of the night?" One of the women asked and lifted her glass and toasted.

"To being completely satisfied tonight." They clicked glasses and drank down the brown liquid and chased it with orange juice.

"Tastes like syrup," Keiko said as her phone indicated that their car was waiting.

"Ladies, thank you." Keiko pulled Everett by the hand and walked out the bar.

"You can get your car tomorrow; I have a special assignment for you tonight." Keiko kissed him seductively as they fell into the backseat of the car.

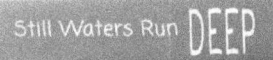

The weekend excursion to Chicago had come to an end, but the memories that Yari and Travis shared would never be forgotten. The first night they enjoyed Chicago style pizza and listening to live Jazz before returning to their suite. They stayed up talking about life in general and then a few pitfalls of the job. They came clean and expressed what pet peeves they had to deal with when they first went undercover and their reaction to the Spencer Snow brothel party before Travis passed out on the couch.

The next day was spent having breakfast with Mandy and an associate who would be present at the opening of the art gallery they had come to attend. They walked The Magnificent Mile and took pictures of the scenic lakefront. When the evening came, they dressed formally. Travis in a Slim-fit deep midnight-blue tuxedo with black satin notch lapels. His bowtie was mixed with hints of purple, medallion and white. Yari in a matching deep blue A-Line Off the Shoulder dress and Burberry Tillington Ankle-Wrap Mules stood out amongst the guests who had been present.

The young couple made lasting impressions with the gallery curator and mayor of Chicago. They took several pictures and made a matching twenty-five-hundred-dollar contribution with Mandy's firm. When the event had concluded, they ventured into the city and found more music venues to their liking. They danced until 3 a.m., until their bodies got tired. They walked the short distance back to the hotel holding hands, and Yari leaning into Travis for support. The lobby was nearly empty as they took the elevator up to their room.

Travis turned the fireplace on before he took a shower first to let Yari take the bath that she said she had been waiting the entire day.

He ate half of a left-over sandwich and drank two glasses of water to hydrate after drinking Hennessey all night.

He had just dozed off when he felt the hand on his chest. He glanced to see Yari wrapped in a hotel towel and her hair wet.

He placed his hand on hers and then pulled her into him on the couch.

The minutes turned into hours and before they fell asleep, in a round-about way, their marriage had been consummated.

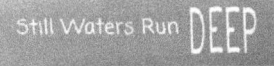

"The team has already found areas to maintain visuals on everyone that comes and goes this weekend. Malcolm and his 'IT' guy have some new accessories that can't be detected so we will have contact with you both." Travis was being briefed by Vania who was happy the undercover work he had done had proven fruitful so far, but they still had to set the hook with Spencer Snow.

"Those pictures are great. Will they let you keep all the

clothes you think?' Vania asked as she set in the condo that Travis and Yari still had to maintain for a few more days.

"I hope so, what woman doesn't like Burberry." Yari smiled and walked into the kitchen with slightly revealing shorts on.

Travis stared a little longer at her. Vania recognized the look but wanted to be certain.

"Being undercover, especially as a married couple and being locked up together, whew I can't even imagine." Vania got up and walked into the kitchen with Yari.

"Your mom and nephews are good. Mama White loves her baby…." Vania paused.

"My ex's sister keeps asking about you T. I told her you were single and available."

Vania saw the slight discomfort in Yari as she walked into the living room and sat down on the couch with Travis, at the opposite end.

"I don't have time for that V.A., we need to finish Spencer off and everything else will fall into place." Travis responded but he felt silly keeping a secret from her, but until this assignment was over; or until Yari and he could determine what 'it' was it would remain their secret.

Vania couldn't stay long as to not blow their cover. She entered under the guise of a potential new tenant in case

Spencer had eyes on them.

"Just lay low, by the end of next weekend this will all be over." Vania grabbed a bottled water before leaving.

Yari made sure that the door locked behind, which it always had. She walked back to the couch and straddled Travis.

"Whatever happens with us, after this, just be honest with me. No lies." She bent into him and kissed him.

"Ditto, Mrs. Carr." He bit her bottom lip before pulling back to stare into her eyes.

"You think she knows" he asked.

Yari moved her hands under his grey sweatpants and shook her head playfully.

"Of course, she knows."

O

The Cabins were connected by small walkways and situated on five acres secluded from the rental properties. They were used only for special events every few months. Spencer Snow had few equals when it came to accounting, and numbers, but his fondness for underage teens was something he could never fully balance.

The guests were mostly those who had been in his inner circle for years, but less than a dozen were new faces like Langdon and Sylvia Carr.

Travis had written the name down of the catering service used at the first get together Spencer had invited them to. With the information, undercover agents were able to mix in as the help.

Lisa appeared to be more cordial, engaging in minor flirtations with some of the other guests present.

"You two, I hoped you'd make it. My colleague in Chicago was very impressed with you both." She greeted them with kisses on the lips and led them onto a wrap-around deck, which connected the cabins.

From the outside, each cabin looked authentically made and blended in with the wooded surrounds.

"I love those frames, but they'd swallow my face." Lisa commented on Yari's eyewear. Courtesy of Malcolm's IT guy. They broadcast what Yari saw with new technology the military developed that couldn't be detected, and they were also fit for communication through the vibrations in the temple portion around her ear. Once it was confirmed that minors were on site, the team hidden in the wooded perimeter would react swiftly.

Lights off in the distance could be seen from the rental area as Yari positioned her body closer to Travis, who leaned over the wooden banister staring at people walking beneath them on the grounds.

"Enjoy what your bodies desire tonight as art enthusiasts. The human body contains so many secrets that I'm sure you have yet to explore. The more inhibitions you lose, the deeper the meaning becomes." Lisa looked Yari up and down. She then traced her fingers up her arm to her shoulder before she departed.

Yari kept a blank expression on her face. The fact of the matter was she had been taken off guard by the woman's slight advances.

"I'm not letting her put one more of her filthy fingers on me." Yari whispered into Travis' ear.

A voice came through her com to 'stay in character'. On cue, they found a server with wine. They would keep a glass for appearances, hopefully this was the moment their undercover work was proving valuable.

They mingled for a considerable amount of time before Lisa pulled them into a second cabin, twice as large as the others, with what appeared to be a lower level built into the ground. It had a security pad on the outside to gain entrance. Lisa entered a code and the door opened.

Spencer sat with a tray of cocaine on a table in front of him. Two young girls sat by his side that had also been at the first event.

"They're of age." Yari kissed Travis' ear to notify the

team not to move in yet. The cocaine was a felonious amount, but that charge would not be enough to pressure him to turn on his boss.

"Sylvia and Langdon Carr, join me, if it's your thing. Tonight, is all about whatever your thing is." He passionately kissed both girls before making them kiss each other.

The undercover agents declined the powdery substance.

"No worries, just more for us." He snorted two more lines, one in each nostril.

A man and woman emerged from a second room and they weren't pleased.

Lisa attended to them, but they pressed forward to where Spencer was seated. Slowly he looked up as the man started to complain directly to him.

"We paid more than we should have, this is supposed to be full service isn't it?"

"Please, if you just come with me…" Lisa tried to get a handle on the situation, but Spencer waved her off.

"You're my guests and if full service is your thing, let me make it right." He offered them to share in his cocaine and disappeared.

"They're ripe just not seasoned." The woman snorted a

line and finally noticed Travis and Yari.

She motioned toward the cocaine.

"Trust us there's a lot less since Spencer offered." Travis was quick on his feet.

"It's hard to find, that thing you just can't live without." Yari directed her comment to the woman.

"Very true, so what's your thing?" The man asked.

"That's too much of a personal question for our first encounter, don't you think?" Yari stared at him intently before bursting out in a smile.

"If you must know, 'purple tigers' do it for us."

Travis shook his head.

"A little too young for us, we've always been fond of 'albino trees' but 'purple tigers' every now and then are added to the menu." The woman had a server bring her an entire bottle of Jack Daniels.

Yari and Travis had been briefed on coded words and phrases that were commonly used to identify victims of pedophiles. Purple Tigers equaled pre-teens and Albino Trees indicated adolescent teens.

Spencer and Lisa returned with two very young-looking girls.

"We apologize for the misunderstanding. To make up

for it." Spencer motioned the girls to the couple who smiled.

A server brought the bottle of whiskey and Spencer picked up the tray of cocaine.

"I will make sure our little angels understand what full service is. Langdon and Sylvia if you excuse me, or join us, whatever your thing is." Spencer entered the same code to gain access to the room the couple had exited originally.

Lisa left Travis and Yari and headed back to check on other guests who had not been invited into Spencer's personal space.

"We're on the move!" Everett's voice was heard in her com.

Commotion erupted all around the property, men and women screaming were drowned out by cars with sirens barreling down both the entrance and exit of the secluded cabins.

"Keep your hands up and don't move. Stay where you are until you are approached, non-compliance is not an option." The swat team leader called out over a bull horn.

Travis and Yari waited for the team to push through to their position. The people in their cabin were panicked, trying to determine ways out without being seen, but there weren't any.

The door opened and Lisa came in only to quickly close

it behind.

"You gotta do something, we didn't come for this!" Guests were screaming at her, along with Yari and Travis.

Lisa pushed through them and entered the room Spencer had gone with the couple and young girls.

"Spencer, oh fuck, get dressed now! The cops are here!" She yelled.

The team had already gotten the access code for Spencer's cabin through Yari's glasses. When they entered, Lisa had just reached the top of the stairs with Spencer behind her with both girls being pulled up the stairs.

"Everybody get down on the ground!" Everett and Cole had their weapons drawn as everyone, including the undercover agents, laid flat on the floor.

Vania found unused linen to wrap around the girls and carried them to safety,

Spencer and Lisa were first to be cuffed and placed into the back of one of the two larger transport vans.

The couple who had emerged upset were next.

Travis and Yari were cuffed and placed in a separate van with the other members of their cabin, including wait staff.

The two undercover agents sat huddled together, grateful to have accomplished their mission, but unsure of what would happen between them next now that their assignment had concluded.

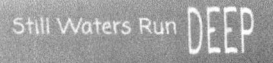

"Spencer there's no way of getting around it. You have to pay for your evil deeds. That could mean spending the rest of your life in jail, marked as a pedophile always wondering who is going to get you, or what day could possibly be your last. It could also mean helping us against your chief employer." District Attorney Scott Calhoun was presenting the scenario with so much riding on his cooperation.

"The Feds are on board…" he continued but Spencer knew the gravity of what he was offering.

"Crusher will have me dead before I'm booked. I'm fucked, and you fucked me." Spencer blurted out.

"Spencer focus, focus. I know it's been a long night, but you haven't been booked yet. We have federal agents ready to take you to safety, but we need you to sign this statement to cooperate in exchange for witness protection as long as what you provide leads to his conviction." Scott finished.

Spencer started biting his nails and fidgeting. There was no viable option he could take that would not have him losing his life, except the deal.

"I want my attorney, wait, no not my attorney, another lawyer who has no ties to Crusher. Yeah, they can't have any connection at all...and...and I want immunity for Lisa. She's dead if I help you and, yeah that's it. But you can't put me anywhere near a jail cell, and don't leave me alone because you know he has cops, cops in his pocket." Spencer pleaded.

The District Attorney pushed the agreement across the table, left the room and was greeted by The Captain and chief of police. Two agents dressed in black fatigues were stationed outside the room Spencer occupied, under strict orders no one go in without being accompanied by the captain.

"Once we get a hold of his financials it's game over. It will link all the corruption in our city and state government. I expect to have pressure placed on my office, but rest assure we will shine like diamonds."

He left Captain Montgomery and the chief of police to speak with each other.

One of the two television sets in the corners of the office were highlighting aspects of the raid.

"Police busted a suspected child sex ring last night. Over thirty people were arrested, and at least a dozen minors who are now being treated for injury and other health related concerns were saved. We will update you with this breaking news as it comes into us." The female anchor then took the program to commercial break.

"Turn that shit off, we are far from done." Captain Montgomery was walking back into his office as he yelled at the office.

"David, cut them slack. This is big and they did a good job," the chief said before she departed.

Travis was in his direct line of sight, so he nodded in approval of the job he had done. Travis returned the gesture.

"Don't let it go to your head." Vania had no problem bringing her partner back to reality.

"Right. Are you hungry?" Travis realized he had not eaten since the previous night.

Vania agreed with him that food was necessary.

"Do you mind if we take mom and the boys something too? I haven't seen them in so long. That's love for checking in on them." Travis thanked her again as they walked the stairs.

"So, where do you want to go?" He didn't want to have to decide, and he also didn't want to drive.

"I don't care really, what do you think Mrs. Carr would have a taste for?"

Vania looked at him with a sly smile and unlocked the doors.

CHAPTER 5
cRYPto and CRYpTS

Commissioner Grahl sat at his desk wondering why he had been placed in this position. His assistant Mario stood at one of the office windows looking out.

"We did what was asked of us, the charges against him have been dropped." His assistant had put thought to the predicament they faced.

"You think he will see it that way? His attorney threatens the DA's office with full disclosure to the press about corrupt cops and a forensic department with a breach. How many cases unravel. Its's not our leverage, it's his." The commissioner watched the incoming call light indicator flash.

"Yes, send her in."

The door opened and the secretary escorted a woman in with a black leather bag hanging loosely from her shoulder. Her lustrous salt and pepper hair extended past her shoulders. The Black pant suit was accented with matching anklets and bracelets. Her frameless glasses showcased her green eyes. Her presence shifted the energy in the office.

"Mr. Commissioner, thank you for seeing me on such short notice." She greeted the older man.

"The pleasure is mine Gwendolyn.

"Can I get anyone anything?" The secretary asked.

"No, no thank you Tracy. Please close...."

"Actually, bring me a cup of Earl Grey tea and bagel with cream cheese. The commissioner will take orange juice and toast." The Secretary left.

"You have to eat Mr. Commissioner; diabetes is a hard disease to manage." She walked to one of the two love seats and sat down with her bag.

"My client has been in an unpleasant mood and I'm sure you know why." She placed her bag onto a small wooden coffee table before crossing her legs.

The secretary returned pushing a small cart with the items ordered and departed.

"Needless to say; my client expects more from this office. Spencer Snow is in federal witness protection, this is something you can determine to be accurate or not." She spread cream cheese onto her bagel and took a bite.

"My hands are tied. The Governor's office has taken an interest and we just need to lay low until we can be smart." The commissioner reached out to take the glass of orange juice that Gwendolyn extended to him.

"It's nearly eleven o'clock and you haven't eaten today. We can't have you getting sick." She took a second bite from her bagel.

The commissioner glanced at his assistant after she revealed she understood he had not eaten yet, knowing his schedule.

He was being monitored more closely than he had known.

"Here's the thing and I'm certain that the lesson has never been lost to either of you." She reached into her black bag and pulled out two files.

"One of the biggest motivating factors is leverage." She passed them each a folder.

Instant concern fell across Mario's face and the blood seemed to drain from both men.

The commissioner was staring at proof of many illegal activities he participated in or covered up; including a cover up from three decades ago involving his partner. If this information got into the wrong hands his career and legacy was over.

"We've had a good partnership over the years. We would hate to end it on a bad note." She thanked him for his time, retrieved her bag and exited the office.

"You've done all you can for her honey. I know you want to give her answers but every time you stick your head out, you put a target on it. You're a good man David John Montgomery but you know I'm right. Just tell her." Johanna Montgomery sat on the bed as her husband looked back at her through the mirror.

He had tried to help the daughter of Officer Kuper, but there were far greater powers at work and each time he got close a roadblock was generated. Over the years he grew in rank and the answers he sought for over thirty years seemed less important.

"You're the smartest woman I know." He pulled a t-shirt on and followed his wife out of their bedroom and downstairs to join the rest of the family.

The aroma of herbs and spices could be smelled throughout the house. His elderly mother lived with them for the past seven years since his father passed. He and his wife built an extension onto their house. It was the only decision that was appropriate because he would not place his mother into a nursing home.

"David set the table." She looked up from the stove after stirring the pasta sauce.

"Mom, that smells soooo good. Thank you for cooking. Did Marissa help at all?" Johanna asked her mother in law.

"Marissa has been sorting through catering options for her wedding, so, no, Mommy, Marissa did not help." Their daughter stood from the sofa with a long list of names of companies.

"Help your father set the table." Johanna directed their daughter before asking her mother in law, "What can I help with?"

"Pour me a glass." She nodded in the direction of one of two bottles of wine sitting in the kitchen island.

"Dad, I know a wedding is the last thing you probably

want to talk about today, but I was thinking..."

"Marissa, your dad has a lot on his mind. You and I can talk about it after dinner." Johanna opened a bottle of red wine.

David looked at his wife and whispered, "Thank you."

The family sat at the dining room table and ate dinner.

Captain Montgomery received a phone call halfway through dinner and excused himself.

Johanna knew it was Laura Kuper-Coates calling for an update.

"Honey, be the honest man you are and tell her," Johanna said lowly as Captain Montgomery walked outside to his enclosed back yard.

"Is Dad okay?" Marissa asked.

"Of course, honey," Johanna responded faster than intended, and when she glanced at David's mother, she knew the elderly woman wasn't buying the answer she gave her daughter.

"Marissa, help me put the food away, and we can look at some of those caterers from your list," the grandmother directed.

Johanna walked to the sliding patio door and watched her husband walk the lighted path in the back yard. They took pride in taking care of their grounds.

He leaned up against the stone barrier separating his neighbor's property.

Johanna knew this was a difficult decision to make, and an even harder conversation to have.

She walked back to the kitchen and returned to the sliding patio door to step outside with her husband. She sat on the patio furniture and waited until he was done with the call.

The look in his eyes was one she had seen less than five times in the thirty-five years they had been together. It was the look of defeat.

She stood up and hugged him. Passed him the bottle of wine and sat down with him at her side.

"This is heavy Jo." He laid his head in her shoulder.

"I know honey. I know."

The only two people who were not being thrown out of the restaurant were his Attorney Gwen and personnel bodyguard. Every other person present received the wrath of Crusher's anger. More than seventy five percent of his wealth had been flagged and placed on hold by authorities. His bitcoin nest egg of over thirty million dollars could not be touched by the authorities.

"Every last one of them are expendable. I want results, not excuses." Derrick walked to his private elevator with Spade and his attorney with him.

He walked straight to his balcony and took in the view of the city.

"Boss, all the shipments are on the road. I learned that Money G and his people are making a play for our Southside connection. I didn't want to make any moves without your knowledge. We've been able to keep the peace, but he's taking advantage of our position. Predators are always hungry." Spade walked onto the balcony behind him.

Crusher inhaled slowly and thought about all the options he could take. It was apparent that with his organization being stressed by law enforcement, laying low would be the wisest. However, he also knew that his greatest asset was still the fear he wielded.

"Send a message, a heavy message."

Spade shook his head in acknowledgement before walking away.

Gwen was sitting at a table looking over paperwork at one of the two sitting areas on his balcony.

Derrick took a lighter from his pocket and sat down. He took hold of a large cigar from the ashtray that was filled with cannabis and lit it.

"We may have to move against some of your assets in the field. They are becoming more of a liability to you and those I represent." She left it at that and handed him two separate forms.

"We transferred the money from the business accounts they didn't find, into three offshore accounts. Your access information is here. There is enough working capital to maintain company business. They expect you to get your house in order." She pulled her hair to one side and reached for Derrick's cigar.

"They have more than eighty-million dollars of mine held up, I've got another thirty-million in crypto. I understand what's at stake. I've made them rich and limited their risk, just remind them of that."

Gwen raised her eyebrows and coughed after inhaling the cannabis.

"They understand their power, you should remember your position." She sat forward and handed him the cigar before sliding files back into her briefcase.

"I would never tell you how to run your organization but a discussion with the mayor seems appropriate under the circumstances." She stood up and took one last look at Derrick and walked off the balcony and out of the loft.

Veronica had her head in the computer when Sheldon walked in. They had gotten a look at Derrick Crusher's financials and had spent the last four days combing through them. It led to him finding out that Derrick Crusher had two large bitcoin accounts in excess of thirty million combined, unfortunately for him, Malcolm found the access code to one and was now in control of over seventeen million dollars.

"Have you ever seen that many commas?" Veronica asked Sheldon upon his entrance. She was linking each money transaction to other accounts to find more connections to his business dealings.

Sheldon seemingly ignored her and walked out.

He walked back to his workstation and retrieved his phone and reentered the office space Veronica occupied.

"Those are a lot of commas." He sat down at a different monitor and double checked some of his findings.

Veronica ignored him and spent the next three hours straining her eyes looking at numbers. She traced several payments made to officers on the force, and city officials. She had only gone through twenty percent of the information, but she knew the importance of it. She closed the computer and slid her chair back to stare at the ceiling.

"Veronica you should leave and rest. You're working almost as much as I am." Sheldon's voice caught her off guard. She had forgotten he had been sitting less than ten feet away.

"Geez, Sheldon." Veronica caught herself from tipping over in her chair.

He grabbed a stack of papers from the printer and walked out of the room they occupied.

She grabbed her cell phone and turned it on. A list of text messages populated along with two missed phone calls.

"Seven o'clock."

The lab was nearly empty, besides Sheldon and two other techs. Veronica read her text messages and saw that her date cancelled because he was stuck at work. In a way she was grateful because she didn't feel a connection and only wanted to pass time.

"Fuck it." She removed her Airpods from her charging case and put them in. She opened another file and dove into the next accounts to generate more bad guys to take down with Crusher.

She lost track of time again until Sheldon tapped her on the shoulder. He had his lab coat in his hand and a strange look on his face.

"You have to leave Veronica, it's after ten and I need you back early in the morning." Sheldon paused and walked closer to the computer.

"These names are to the account holders?"

"Uh, yeah. I've only been through about twenty percent of all the data, but there are some corrupt cops on the list." Veronica wasn't sure why Sheldon had moved her to the side so that he could look closer at the screen.

"You have no idea, do you?" He reached into his pocket for his cell phone.

"Clearly, I do not." she paused,

"Is that what excitement looks like on your face." Veronica waited for a response, but he was speaking with Malcolm about an account that was tied to the mayor.

"Yeah, Veronica uncovered it. She's still here, yes." Sheldon shook his head and got off the phone.

"So, we have to stay a little longer. Malcolm is on his way in. This is going to be a long night; you should've taken my advice. Now, you're in the game." He left her sitting in the room.

Veronica felt proud that her work was going to make a difference. She walked out of the room and into a small break area and brewed fresh coffee. She saw an unopened box of donuts on the table and grabbed the entire container before walking back to the computer workstation.

Malcolm entered the lab and spoke with Sheldon as they walked to where Veronica was dipping donuts into her coffee.

"So, what do we have?" Malcolm pulled a chair up and started looking at the names linked to the Crusher accounts for payment transfer.

He scanned down the screen and began jotting down information in a small notepad.

"Veronica this is excellent work. If I could give you a raise I would." Malcolm left the lab as quickly as he entered.

Veronica, perplexed, watched him move quickly out the lab.

Sheldon took a donut from the box and waited for her to turn her computer off. He opened the lab door for her and turned off the lights before the door locked behind them.

Everett and Cole walked up the stairs of city hall with the morning sun pitched at their back. The chief of police confirmed that the mayor would be in his office this Friday morning, he had a city budget that needed to be finalized and would be present at the committee overseeing the funds.

The mayor needed to be questioned as to why three of the business his family owned had received money traced back to accounts associated with Derrick Crusher.

"Speak of the devil." Cole nodded to a group of men exiting the stone washed building.

Derrick Crusher was speaking with one of the men in his entourage when he made eye contact with the detectives.

The groups stared at each other in passing.

Cole and Everett reached the entrance as Derrick and his posse got into two separate vehicles waiting at the curb.

"The audacity. His world is crumbling all around him, and he acts like he still owns the city." Cole walked ahead of Everett. He was ready to put the mayor to question with the undeniable proof of a connection.

"I'll give you a call tonight." The commissioner of Police was walking out of the mayor's office.

They made eye contact with Everett before Cole was greeted by the secretary.

"Mr. Mayor, good morning. We have a couple of quick

questions for you. We can take up ten minutes of your time?" Everett greeted the elected official without acknowledging the commissioner. Cole stared the commissioner in the face and shook his head.

"Do you have something to say to me detective?" the commissioner asked.

Cole smiled at him and nodded his head before replying.

"Soon."

Cole continued into the mayor's office closing the office door behind him.

Papers were scattered on the floor, and the furniture had been moved from the indication of a chair laying on its side.

"Small whirlwind ran through here." Cole smirked as his phone buzzed with another California number. It all made sense if one of the mayor's morning guests was Derrick Crusher and his crew; and since the commissioner had been in attendance, it only solidified what they also knew about his dealings with the criminal boss.

"What is it detectives, my schedule is pretty full today?" He turned the chair upright and picked the remaining papers from the floor.

"What's your connection with Derrick Crusher?"

Everett charged in.

The mayor turned to face them. A slight hesitation proceeded his answer.

"There is none, now get the fuck out of my office! This is inappropriate!" He lashed out.

Everett pulled the file from his bag and threw it on his desk. He watched as the mayor read the receipts of money transfers into his business entities.

"Not inappropriate at all," Cole added.

"I have no idea what this is." He continued his denial.

"These transactions are sums of money being deposited into your business accounts and are linked to Derrick Crusher."

The mayor walked to his desk and sat down in his black leather chair.

"What did he want with you this morning?" Cole asked a follow up question.

The mayor seemed to have more than one thing on his mind and was slow to answer.

"Mr. Crusher wanted to express his concern that as a tax paying, law abiding citizen who donates to both political parties; he feels the city is trying to upend his life. He wanted to know what I was going to do about keeping citizens such as himself safe." The mayor stood up picked the file up.

"I'm going to have to have my people look into this. I'll get to the bottom of it. Now please. If you will, I have a budget meeting to attend. The city's money can't be wasted." He motioned for them to leave.

Cole and Everett walked out of his office and through city hall knowing they had baked the cookies. Now they had to be patient to see which one would crumble first.

The day passed with small amounts of information trickling into the team. After exhausting their current leads, Everett excused the team earlier than expected.

Malcolm had his music playing loudly. His neighbor's homes were situated far enough away, that he could barely make out the outline of their houses. He had spent the entire week using a program he created to break into Derrick Crusher's encrypted files. Once he had gotten in, he found the account access to Derrick's Bitcoin account.

Malcolm logged into the cryptocurrency account and stared at the dollar amount. The changed credentials would allow him, and only him access. His IT guy found a backdoor into Derrick's encryption on his computer where he stored the account number and Malcolm did the rest.

"What do you want? What do you want you big ol' baby? Oh, and you want whatever Ditto want's?"

His rottweiler sat in the door frame while his Lab-Pitbull mix tried to push past him and into the room.

Malcolm logged out of the account and walked into the front portion of his home. He stared out of his window onto his great lawn area. He appreciated the seclusion he had found ten years ago after breaking it off with his fiancé.

"Okay, okay." He walked through a living room area and opened a sliding glass door to allow their exit.

His phone rang.

"Cole, what's good, brother?" Malcolm walked into the kitchen to retrieve a beer.

"It's about time we get a moment... Yeah... Yeah, okay, I'll meet you guys there." Malcolm poured dog food into two large bowls and replenished his dog's water.

He took a shower and changed into a casual outfit with his signature flair before walking back to the living room patio.

"Ditto... Buttons, come on. Come on! Let's go!"

His dogs came running back with their tails wagging.

"Daddy's got a surprise birthday party to go to. You guys can eat-eat." Both dogs ran to their respective bowls.

Malcolm took a last look in one of the full mirrors in his home, grabbed some cash, and walked into his four-car garage. He walked past a 2016 White Range Rover and one of 318 Mustang Shelby GT500KR convertibles made. Malcolm came to rest in front of a 1960 Smoked Grey Mercedes-Benz Roadster.

"Lenny, will you be my date tonight?" He opened the door and started the car.

"I know... I know. We haven't been out in so long." He used a remote to open his garage and turned the lights on.

"I promise no one could ever take your place." He shifted into gear and pressed on the gas.

When Vania walked into the restaurant after leaving the Jiu Jitsu studio with Ed and Lynn, the married co-owners of the gym, she vowed to accept whatever they wanted to do in celebration of her birthday. She had not really celebrated in years, not since her cousin had been killed. They shared the same birthday, and it brought unpleasant memories of him up.

The downtown restaurant club was full as usual and even as she fought against the birthday dinner, that the married couple made reservations, or at minimum the wait wouldn't be long.

A man carrying drumsticks walked towards a stage where live music would be played later in the night.

The greeter smiled and walked them through the main dining room into a larger room meant for groups. When the doors were slid back, Vania was genuinely surprised to see members of her team along with friends from forensics. Her roommate and Yari gave her hugs, and Travis held a present in one hand and a glass of wine in the other for her.

"Happy birthday, V.A." He handed her both items.

Vania felt an overwhelming amount of emotion that she couldn't contain and started to cry with her head in his chest.

"Vivi, it's ok. We can celebrate his memory too," Lynn said while Vania got herself together.

After the moment passed, dinner was served, and the celebration got lively as a house band started playing their first set.

Some of those sitting at the bar moved to the small dance area.

Vania pulled Travis to the side and explained why she had gotten emotional earlier.

"It just gets me some kind of way, I hope I didn't mess

your shirt up."

"V.A. I get it, but tonight, let's celebrate your birthday and his memory." Travis touched her on the hand while Everett bought the first round of drinks, reminding them all to take ride shares home if they couldn't drive.

"I love each and every one of you, but get a drunk driving citation, and I will fire you."

They toasted to Vania's birthday and then Yari, and Veronica pulled her out to the floor to dance.

"She looks happy," Travis said in reference to his partner.

Malcolm put his hand on the young detective's shoulder and motioned with drink in hand towards the three women dancing.

"They all look happy." Malcolm moved in step with the music and made his way to the trio to dance with them.

Yari looked at Travis, and shortly after, he also joined them.

The celebration was winding down. Everett and Sheldon had already left, along with the married couple.

"No one is driving home except me tonight." Malcolm stood at the bar with the group waiting to cash out.

"Why do you get to drive home Mr. Malcolm X?" Vania

shook her head loosely like she didn't know why he was giving himself a pass.

"It's your birthday, and you're drunk, so that's an extra birthday gift. I've killed people for less. Now everybody pull out your phones and get to Ubering." He smiled as he waved down the bartender.

"Can you put everything on my tab and one more round for everyone except me?"

"What kind of shot do you want?" The bartender pulled out seven shot glasses.

"V.A., nightcap shot, what's it going to be?" Veronica leaned over Vania's shoulder.

"Purple Hooters with Goose." She started dancing at the bar with Veronica.

"I love you, guys. Thank you for helping me celebrate my 21st birthday."

The group looked at her, and then they all burst out laughing.

"Twenty-one, my ass." Cole made his way to the bar counter.

"Seven purple hooters, happy birthday again." The bald bartender placed the tray of drinks down.

"We only needed six," Malcolm said as he handed each person a shot glass of liquid.

"The extra one is for her, from me." He winked at Vania.

"Hey, Romeo, can I get a Steiner glass of water? Cole asked jokingly.

"Thank you." Vania lipped to the bartender.

"Make that two glasses of water, please," Travis added.

"Thank God tomorrow is Sunday because I will not be setting my alarm for anything or anyone," Yari said as they lifted their shot glasses.

"My life has been pretty strange since joining this team, but I wouldn't trade it in for the world. Thank you." Vania raised her glass.

"Happy birthday, boriqua!" Rosey yelled out, and they took the shot.

Malcolm took care of the bill before Cole followed him outside to take a long look at 'Lenny'.

"Men and their cars." Veronica stared at Cole a little longer than she intended, but the liquor was bringing up memories.

"Let that go," Yari said and checked how long before her ride would arrive.

"I guess I'm going to head out myself partner, see if I

can catch a ride with one of the fellas and not have to pay to get dropped off at home." He hugged her and said goodbye to the other two.

"T, why don't you ride with Yari? It's on the way. Veronica is staying with us tonight, and you guys don't stay far from each other." V.A. said slowly not to slur her words.

Travis didn't answer right away. He wasn't sure if Yari wanted to have company since they had not been alone with each other since they broke cover.

"That's fine, but we have to go, they're pulling up." Yari hugged the women one last time and walked out.

Vania, buzzed, winked her eye at Travis who then turned and followed Yari out of the restaurant club.

"Our ride is five minutes out. Use the restroom if you must." Vania's roommate returned and asked where Travis had gone.

"Rideshare with Yari; they just left." Veronica walked towards the restroom with Vania behind.

Vania had not told anyone that she knew about her partner and Yari, which included her roommate who was interested in Travis. When they returned from the bathroom, three more shots were waiting.

"For the road," her roommate said as they tilted back the drinks.

When they walked out of the building, the parking lot was less full. The cool night breeze ran across their exposed skin, and they dove into the back seat of the Acura waiting to take them home.

After their day off, the team got back to building a concrete case against Crusher and anyone else involved in his corruption. City Hall was breathing down Captain Montgomery's back, coupled with the commissioner's assistant paying the captain two unscheduled visits.

The Feds were cooperating with local enforcement being ensured that any and all information of the case would be shared for the federal charges waiting to be filed.

"I have a headache. Clark, you've got something in your desk to help?" Captain Montgomery approached Everett's teams' area after speaking to Jack and his partner.

"Extra strength *Tylenol* or ibuprofen?" Everett reached into his desk drawer pulling out two containers.

"Give me the ibuprofen." Everett opened the bottle and positioned the pills to pour into the captain's hand, but the captain took the whole bottle.

"What do we have?" he asked.

The entire team was working hard. Travis and Vania had morning interviews with the officers tied to Derrick Crusher's financials. Their interviews were being conducted in a remote area the chief of police had secured. Cole and Malcolm were piecing together a few leads that Malcolm's IT guy brought to light.

Everett looked at the captain and nodded his head towards the captain's office to indicate it was better to speak on it away from the bullpen. Although many of the moles were being rooted out, it was best not to take chances.

Everett followed him into his office and closed the door.

"The mayor and commissioner are toast. Forensics has conclusive evidence that is undeniable. Friday when we met with him at City Hall, Commissioner Grahl was walking out. They're rattled. This is the closest we've had Crusher in our crosshairs, and I won't miss this shot." Everett handed the captain the file he had in hand.

Captain Montgomery winced and rubbed his temples.

"Between this case, and a wedding for my very spoiled, second daughter, my head feels like it's going to explode." The captain took three pills and swallowed them, followed by a big swig of water.

"The wedding isn't for another six months, I thought." Everett had a puzzled look on his face.

"Clark, you have a daughter. Start saving money now, they turn into creatures that you don't recognize..." he paused as he sat down at his desk.

"I need you to bring this home. Men like Crusher become more dangerous than an animal backed into a corner. Cornered animals will tear down everything and everyone that gets in their way of survival. Crusher has the power to set this city back decades."

Everett shook his head in agreement and then added to the conversation, hoping he wouldn't get chewed out for indirectly disobeying an order.

"So, when we got into the financials, there was some information... dirt... that Crusher held over people. One of those files may indicate that the commissioner was in fact implicated in a cover up from the case that's followed you for over thirty years."

Captain Montgomery looked at Everett, the expression on his face wasn't easily readable. He took a deep breath and asked what was found.

Everett stood up and pulled a USB from his front jean pocket.

"If this is accurate, it implicates a powerful family." Everett handed it USB to the captain.

The captain took another sip of water and slouched into his chair.

"Who else has seen this?"

Everett advised him only Malcolm and Cole.

"Well Sheldon too because he discovered it, but it's contained."

The captain nodded his head and thanked Everett before dismissing him from his office.

"Clark, you have a visitor in the break room." Jack called out.

Everett wasn't expecting anyone so as he walked into the break room he was taken by complete surprise.

"I'm kinda new to this, I hope I haven't overstepped." Keiko had brought him lunch.

The smile across Everett's face couldn't be contained. He walked to the table she had placed the bags of food and kissed her.

"So, you do have a life outside this job." Jack said after pouring himself a mug of coffee.

"This is a pleasant surprise. Normally I'm out running leads down."

"Well, it was a chance I was willing to take." She smiled at him.

Everett opened the bags and pulled out containers.

"Buffalo Chicken Sandwich with fries for me, and a steak with baked potato and salad for you." Keiko sat down and pulled utensils from the bag.

"Stop staring, you're embarrassing me." She blushed.

Everett's cell phone rang as he took his first bite. It was Cole.

Everett took a second bite of his sandwich as he answered the phone.

"What's up, Cole?

Everett's eyes lit up as he stared at Keiko.

She saw the concern on his face as he shook his head listening to the information Cole was relaying.

"Yeah ok, I'll be there shortly." He ended the call.

Keiko took a fork of his salad and closed her box.

"Trust me, I understand." She put her food container back into the bag she carried in and kissed him on his cheek.

"I'm so sorry, the body of a person of interest has been found and I have to..."

Keiko looked him in his eyes and repeated.

"I understand, but you can walk me out." Everett stood up and placed his food in the breakroom refrigerator. He took an ink pen and wrote his name on the box.

When they walked out of the breakroom and toward the elevator, the officers in the bullpen started whistling.

"Clark." A voice called out in reference to how beautiful Keiko was.

"She outranks everyone in this building, so shut your traps." Everett shook his head in jest as the elevator door opened.

Keiko stopped and pulled Everett closer for a passionate kiss as everyone looked on.

"That should give them something to build rumors."

The elevator door closed with Everett staring at her.

Everett pulled up to the crime scene and got out of his car. Malcolm was speaking to members of the forensics team who held computer tablets in their hands. He saw Cole speaking with uniformed officers in the garage of the victim.

As he approached the garage, he noticed the bits of glass marked by Malcolm's team. The victim's body hung slightly from the driver's side door that was ajar.

Instinctively Everett looked up at the house to see if any security measures were in place. There were none.

"Assistant to the commissioner." Cole met him as he walked into the garage.

Everett bent down and looked at the murder victim. There was one shot to the right torso, in addition to one entering the body into the right temple area.

"Hmph." Everett looked at the key fob resting between the feet of the victim on the floor beneath the brake pedal.

"A couple was out for a morning jog and saw the garage open and didn't think anything of it, until they were walking back to cool down. That's when they saw the body." Cole kept bringing his partner up to speed.

Everett thought it made sense because the house sat in a cul-de-sac and the angle would've blocked them from seeing the body.

"It looks like the perp sat on the passenger side. From the trajectory I'd say front seat, and since no one reported sounds of gunshots being fired, I'd bet a silencer was used." Cole nodded at Malcolm who was entering the garage.

"Time of death between midnight and four a.m.

Gunshot wound to the head was fatal." Malcolm advised them both.

"The house has been ransacked; computer devices are nowhere to be found." Malcolm walked both detectives back into the victim's home.

Everett saw the cords still hanging from the wall outlets where devices had been plugged in. A briefcase had its contents hanging out.

"This is a mess. I wonder if they found what they were looking for." Everett said out loud to no one in particular. He walked further into the home, checking the bedrooms and basement area. All the drawers had been removed and tossed, the mattresses and box springs destroyed. The basement was bare except for a washer and dryer. He stood in the middle of the basement formulating that this was a message being sent to the commissioner.

Movement from behind the water tank had him reach for his gun, until he saw the Egyptian Mau Cat with black collar and silver bell. Everett kneeled and the cat walked to him and smelled his hand before rubbing her fur up against him.

He picked it up and walked back up the stairs.

"I was wondering where the cat was. There's a food bowl and cans of cat food in the cupboard." Cole touched the cat on its head. He had always been an animal person but had not owned any since his early college years.

"We will have this processed in next few hours. The body's been taken back for Sheldon to start on." Malcolm was staring out of the front window of the home when both detectives approached with the cat.

"This is Ausar." Everett made the introduction.

Malcolm shook his head at the detectives after reading the name on the collar.

"That's fitting." He smirked.

Cole looked at him strangely and then at Everett. Everett shook his head because he didn't understand what reference Malcolm was making.

"Come on guys, Ausar? Osiris, the Egyptian Lord of the Underworld." Malcolm rubbed the cat and walked out the room.

"What the fuck do you mean calm down, don't tell me to calm down. The coroner has his body on a cold slab right now. This is all going to hell." The commissioner was speaking to the mayor about his assistant's body being found. The pressure was squeezing them, and Derrick Crusher was that pressure.

He poured himself a shot of bourbon and repeated it

two more times after drinking the first.

"I told you years ago when we had him dead to center on the death of that family, we should've wiped his legs out from under him, didn't I? You gave your assistant power and he pissed some people off. We can't be certain, who, at this point." The mayor walked to the mini bar in his office and poured himself a Scotch.

"What I am certain of, is the detectives have proof of my family business accepting questionable money. There are layers they still have to peel back and make certain under the letter of the law that everything is accurate. They aren't there yet, but they are very close." The mayor drank the scotch and moved to his sitting area.

"I have a few connections in the federal prosecutor's office overlooking all of this. I will have a better idea after touching base. For now, mourn the loss of your assistant. Issue a public statement that you will be taking a few days off while going through a close tragedy."

The commissioner agreed that it was the best course of action to take.

"But what about the chief? She's, got her hand all over this investigation and the DA is pressing forward with the charges against him." The commissioner still had concerns.

"The is the least of our worries. She will be handling questions about the police force as the media gets wind of the corruption under her watch." The mayor sat back.

"You mean our watch. They elected you to fix the problem, Mr. Mayor."

The mayor showed no additional concern when he responded.

"Politics will take care of her."

The office door opened, and Gwen was being escorted in by the secretary.

"Gentlemen."

The door closed behind her and she walked directly to the mini bar and poured two glasses of scotch, and one of bourbon. She walked the drinks back to the men.

"You received the gift my employer left for you this morning." Gwen said adjusting her long red hair over her shoulder.

"A gift, a gift is that what you call it!" The commissioner's tone showed that he was offended by her choice of words.

She raised her eyebrows and took a sip from her glass.

"Yes, a gift. You are able to sit across from me and have a conversation, are you not?" she paused to let the bit of information sit in.

From the look in the commissioner's eyes the point had been made, the murder victim could have been him.

"I usually don't drink this early in the afternoon, but these matters are of grave concerns. I'm sure you both understand. No one wants to have their legs wiped out from under them. To be honest, it sounds pretty offensive at the least...and painful."

The office door opened again. The secretary returned with three large pizza boxes.

"Thank you so much, you can put one down on the table and the rest is for the office." Gwen smiled at the secretary and asked if the sodas had been included with the order. The secretary affirmed that she had to make a second trip.

The mayor stared at the commissioner not understanding what was taking place in his office.

"Thanks for the pizza, but we both have to..."

"You both will sit here and tell me your plan, besides speaking with your federal connections and you issuing a statement. Eat the fucking pizza or not, I don't give a shit, but it's the last bit of kindness either two of you will see unless you handle the problems at hand."

Gwen smiled as the secretary returned with the beverages.

She stood up and opened the pizza box and put two slices on a plate.

"Do you guys want any or not?" she asked as the

secretary opened a two-liter of Sprite

"You're a lifesaver." Gwen acknowledged with a wink before the secretary departed for the final time.

"David, I can't stop trying to figure out what happened to my father. I have supported law enforcement since before I could walk, and I still have faith in the system, even though it has not been kind in return." Laura Kuper-Coates was being a matter of fact. It wasn't meant to challenge Captain Montgomery.

He understood the determination it took for Laura to pursue the truth. He attributed it to her father.

"Laura, I can't go into specifics, but more things are coming into the light. The rank and file have been under attack from within and from the outside. Just tread lightly. There have been two deaths we are looking into that may tie it all together." He waited to hear if she needed to speak with him about anything else before they ended the call.

"Honey let your guys do their job. You've learned more in the past two months than you have in the past twenty-years. Tomorrow I am going to pay off your daughter's wedding dress and mark it off the list. We have been blessed with a good life. I may have had to worry a little more than most wives, but I wouldn't change it for the world.' She kissed him on his shoulder and walked into the den.

Captain Montgomery couldn't stop thinking about Officer Kuper since he was informed of the progress Malcolm had made along with the two senior detectives.

The doorbell rang and he saw from the camera situated above his front door that a delivery package had been left. He walked to the door and retrieved the package.

"D.J. your wife said you've been getting migraines again." Captain Montgomery's mother entered the kitchen and addressed him by his childhood nickname.

"Yeah, mom. Work has had a different kind of stress waiting on me when I get in and when I leave. Everything is going to be ok." He pulled the tape from one side of the box, before realizing the sides had pieces of tape.

"Daddy, thank you so much for paying my dress off!" Marissa came barreling into the kitchen followed by his wife again.

"Yeah, yeah."

His daughter wrapped her arms around him.

"I love you!"

"I love you too." He said lightly as the box opened,

Inside the box was another box that had a negative sign in red on it.

"Honey, why don't you take mom and Rissa into the den and I'll be in to watch the movie too." He made eye contact with his wife.

"What's inside the box dad?" his daughter asked and pulled the smaller box from his hand.

He reached for it but was too late as she opened it.

An awkward silence ensued.

"Who would mail you their badge to quit. A face-to-face resignation has more dignity." She handed it to her father and went back to the den.

Baby you ok?" his wife asked.

Captain Montgomery saw the name on the shield and knew the stakes had just been raised. He called the chief and requested support for his family, and the families of those investigating the case. He wasn't taking any chances. What normally would be off limits, was not.

He had Everett and Cole drive out to his home to formulate a plan, and the only problem was he didn't know how the pieces were being moved across the board.

Derrick sat alone in the restaurant after they closed between the lunch and dinner crowds to prep. The few items that the mayor was able to get back from evidence were necessary and none more important than an encrypted tablet with access to his cryptocurrency accounts. His passwords had been placed in secret programs for an extra level of security.

Spade was walking from the back-kitchen area with a plate of southern fried chicken and red velvet waffles.

"The institution is going to want their money back, and it's better to take care of them before any interest can be exacted. I'm going to transfer the two million back, and once the next shipment is distributed, we'll make double that back." Derrick reached down and took a chicken leg from the plate.

Spade spread butter on the waffles, followed by a massive amount of syrup.

"I haven't had shit to grub on since, damn since lunch yesterday," Spade said, taking his first portion.

Derrick glanced up and shook his head. He took another bite of chicken after moving money from one account back into The Institution's account. It was an amount he would have liked to have kept, but business was business. He had only taken one front in his life, and that was from his predecessor, who taught him the way of the world—the real world. Where power was the only true consequence.

"The commissioner needs to resign, and we move the deputy chief into a position that moves him up the chain faster than we predicted. I can speak with Gwen to be certain what levers to pull on to minimize additional exposure. We had enough exposure with my name and face being pumped out into the media. Make sure they know that was a one-time pass. I don't pay them to not do their jobs." Crusher closed the one cryptocurrency account to check his other.

"I'll have them do everything short of retracting the stories. You were questioned and released without any charges being drawn against you, boss. I can make a trip out right..." Spade held the last few words in his mouth when he recognized the emotion that quickly surfaced with his boss.

"A motherfucker stole from me!" Derrick stared at the tablet screen.

"Boss?" Spade put his fork down.

"I had close to twenty million in a separate account and now I have no access to it. My password doesn't work. The only way to get into these types of accounts are with a passcode and only I know them." Derrick went back and double checked the account that still had a little over ten million dollars in it.

"The Institution wouldn't move against me like this, not yet anyway. Someone who had access to my shit, violated me. Find out the names of anyone who could hack a cryptocurrency account. Find them and keep them alive until the money is transferred back. Then we erase them and anyone associated with them from existence. Skill levels like this are one in five million." Derrick watched Spade as he motioned to the guards standing in remote areas of the restaurant. His personal bodyguard was the closest thing he had to a friend. He had saved Derrick's life more than seven times over the years, even taking two bullets meant for him.

"Spade!" Derrick called out to his bodyguard.

"Yeah, boss."

Derrick stood and walked to him. He put his hands on his shoulders and looked him in the eye.

"Turn over every rock until you locate who stole from me." Derrick handed Spade the plate with chicken on it.

"Eat this shit on the way out and find my money." Derrick needed him focused and a hungry stomach wouldn't provide that.

"So, you think you'll be able to get me a position with salary and benefits?" Avery said excitedly. He had fallen in love with programming before the age of ten and had learned his advanced computer skills from his parents, who were now serving out the last few years after being caught hacking federal government agencies.

Malcolm heard the enthusiasm in his IT guy's voice over the phone, and it made him smile.

"Full benefits for sure. I tried to write an additional fifty thousand for your position, but they only gave me a little under forty-grand. Are you okay with that?" Malcolm stared out into his front yard, watching his dogs play in the water sprinklers set on a timer.

He left Sheldon in charge of the lab for the final few hours of the workday. Malcolm had travelled to Cincinnati and Cleveland in one day to have hand delivered the results of what they found from the cases Gene, the former lab specialist, had compromised.

Less than five cases had evidence that would be thrown out in a court of law if those cases were to be reviewed. He understood his department would get a target on its back from people wanting to shift blame, but as he looked over the case files, most of the criminals were low level associates of Crusher's organization. From their criminal records, he had no doubt they would be arrested again.

"Are there bonuses?" Avery asked.

"Bonuses, shit, I may buy you lunch every now, and then, hell, no, ain't no bonuses." Malcolm laughed before pouring out half of a bottle of warm beer.

"When can I start?" Avery had been waiting for a chance to join Malcolm's team. Malcolm was one of the few people in his life that he felt he could learn from.

"We will onboard you in the next thirty days, but I still need you until then."

Malcolm walked back to his patio and allowed his dogs back in while listening to Avery's excitement through the phone.

"I've always wanted to get into law enforcement. If I do a good job do you think the Feds will let me work on some of their stuff eventually..." Avery paused as there was a knock on his door.

"Avery Holmes?'

Malcolm heard a husky voice on the other line.

"Yeah, I'm Avery..."

"Get in the fucking house and shut up!" Several voices were heard after he verified his identify.

"I hear you're a hacker who likes to break into people's shit."

The phone went dead.

Malcolm called back, and it rang once and went to voicemail.

Malcolm grabbed a set of keys from his hooks holding them in place. He ran to the garage and got into his SUV while calling Everett.

The call went to voicemail.

Malcolm pulled out of his garage as he called Everett again and left a voicemail.

"Meet me at my IT guys address. Something bad, and I need you." He hung up and called Cole, who answered.

"Yo, what's up are you trying to go on the prowl tonight?" Cole's voice was light.

"Hey, I need you to meet me at 942 Maryland. I think Crusher's people found my IT guy," Malcolm said as he sped out of his development and onto a county highway that ran into a major interstate.

"Wait, what. Your IT guy… Avery?" Cole asked with concern in his voice, he was trying to get the pieces to fit.

"Yeah, Avery. He was the one that broke through most of the security on Crushers' computers. He opened a tablet for me, and I was able to access one of Crusher's cryptocurrency accounts," Malcolm shared.

"Cryptocurrency? So, it wasn't listed in the other financials they put a hold on?" From the sound shifting on Cole's phone, Malcolm could tell Cole was already in route.

"I'll get a hold of who I can and meet you." They hung up.

Malcolm arrived before Cole and Vania did.

Avery's home was tossed with a few blood splatters near the door.

"They took him. Those motherfuckers took him. There's surveillance cameras…" Malcolm paused, realizing that all of Avery's computers and servers were missing.

"Who could have taken him?" Travis asked as he appeared in the living room without anyone noticing his arrival.

"It's my fault, all my fault." Malcolm walked the house looking for other clues.

"Avery opened up some of Crusher's devices that needed his special touch. Some of those accounts are valuable." Cole left it at that, and anything else was information no one needed yet.

"Forensics will be here shortly. Malcolm stay here and process what you can. I'll take the team to his restaurant and see what we can find." Everett walked in.

"The captain received the commissioner assistant's badge in the mail earlier. He issued protective orders for all of us starting tomorrow. Malcolm if I can speak with you." Everett motioned Malcolm into another portion of the home.

"This isn't your fault. Avery was doing his job and we will find him. You have to be on your game with so much at stake."

Malcolm acknowledged Everett's words, but he knew it was his fault. He had been the one to recruit Avery out of college and pay him from his own pocket.

The team walked out together leaving Malcolm inside.

A small white van pulled onto the street, and three forensic technicians emerged.

"Crusher has escalated his attacks we have to tread cautiously." Everett got his car and drove to the new restaurant club that Derrick Crusher opened with his team behind him.

CHAPTER SIX
a beginning

"We're here to speak with the owner. Let him know that we're here." Everett and the team walked into the restaurant and sat down at one of the two empty tables left. The dinner crowd was in full swing. The upscale restaurant club was the newest thing to do in Columbus, Ohio.

Travis noticed a few councilmen sitting together

enjoying food. He nodded in their direction.

"You think they know they're supporting a kingpin and murderer?"

"Yeah, they know." Cole watched a few patrons glance their way as their badges hung loosely from their necks.

The manager of the establishment walked to their table.

"Officers, we have a very busy evening, and unless you've made reservations or have a warrant, I'm going to have to ask you to leave." He spoke with a moderate accent.

A second person approached him, and he spoke in German.

"Get rid of them, there are to be no pigs in the establishment, especially non-paying ones" was the rough translation.

"Is he here?" Cole asked.

"Excuse me?" The unknown man looked at Cole.

"Mr. Crusher, is he here?" Vania asked this time. She noticed his earpiece.

"We have guests waiting for this table, and I need to ask you to leave." He spoke in English to the detectives before speaking again in German to the manager.

"He will send them another message soon." He smiled towards the team without realizing that Vania could understand and speak German perfectly.

"I think you have it wrong. We are here to give him a message..." she paused and switched back to English.

"You can speak with us right now or have the entrance of your establishment shut down while we investigate if everyone here is legal to work. If those suppliers we saw unloading trucks before we walked in have any illegal workers...." Everett interjected and got to what mattered most.

"We understand your boss has run into some financial problems. Do you understand now, or should I have her say it in German, Spanish, or Russian?"

Cole and Everett watched the back doors to the kitchen area open, and they were asked to follow Spade.

"Detectives." The bodyguard emerged from behind the door and walked them to the elevator which lead to the second level night club. It was much quieter than the restaurant.

Derrick Crusher was sitting at the bar by himself, but he had six guards at advantage points should the conversation go wrong.

"I don't have time for idle threats, consider this—an exchange of information. A one-time offer detectives." He turned his bar stool to face them.

"Where is Avery?" Cole asked straight forwardly.

"Where the fuck is my money? It wasn't included in the funds on hold so that means someone stole from me. If that's the case, I'd like to report a crime." He stared at Everett.

Spade walked and spoke to one of the guards.

Everett knew this was posturing. Derrick would not risk additional exposure, nor would he gamble knowing the odds were not in his favor should any escalated shooting take place.

"My partner asked you where Avery is."

"I asked you where the seventeen million dollars are that wasn't reported. If I'm the monster you all believe me to be and you think I have something to do with this Avery person, how long do you think he would remain alive? Hypothetically, if he was involved in stealing millions of my hard-earned money, what do you think is happening to him right now?" Derrick stood up and walked towards the team.

Cole took a step toward him, but Everett put his arm up to prevent him from escalating the situation.

"Crusher, let me make one thing clear." Everett closed the distance between him and the criminal kingpin. He stood face to face with him.

"If anything happens to Avery, anything at all, your team...." Everett pointed at each one of them present stationed around the club,

"Will never see us coming." He finished by whispering the last bit in Crusher's ear. Everett took a step back before finishing.

"Thanks for your time." Everett motioned his team to follow him as it was time to leave.

"Never, detective?" Crusher called out as they stepped into the elevator. Everett pressed the button down and answered.

"Like a thief in the night."

"I found two foreign prints at his house. I have two specialists canvassing the area and speaking with neighbors who have exterior cameras. If we can just see the footage around the time of the abduction." Malcolm was distressed that he had not thought about protecting Avery against threats like this. He felt more panicked than he had in years.

"I should've given him the location technology I used for Yari's glasses with Spencer Snow. I've got it in my belt and glasses. I had to make sure it worked before putting it into the field. I was shortsighted, and now these animals have him." Malcolm finished as Sheldon brought back reports from the few samples, they ran tests on.

"The particles are specs of industrial paints. Once the composition is broken down further, we will have a manufacturers lead. Other than that..."

"To hell with other than that, find me something that we can work with." Malcolm stormed out of the forensics lab with his technicians and Everett's team watching.

He walked the hallways before deciding to get fresh air. He walked outside of the precinct, and that's when he got a phone call from a number he didn't recognize.

"Yeah, how can I help you?" His voice reflected his irritation.

"Malcolm, Malcolm..." A loud cough seemed to form his name before Malcolm heard a thud and agonizing moan.

"I don't know anything about that..." Avery's voice called out through the cell.

"Avery, Avery!" Malcolm's voice escalated back into the cell phone.

A second man's voice had replaced Avery and took no time advising Malcolm that Avery had shared something with them.

"Malcolm, we understand you can give back what was stolen." The voice was cold and sterile.

Malcolm listened as he returned inside the building quickly. He opened the door to his lab and made eye contact with Veronica. He motioned for her to run a trace on the call. He hoped to pinpoint a location the call was being made from.

"Yeah, for sure I can get the money back to you. Let me know where I can find Avery and we can make the exchange then." Malcolm tried to keep the caller on the other end. He listened intently and could hear whimpering before he heard Avery scream out.

"Don't do it! They'll kill me and you!" Malcolm heard a second voice that he was familiar with, and he felt a sudden burst of fear for Avery.

"Shut his ass up!"

Avery screamed, and then the background noise went silent.

"I swear if anything happens to him, you won't see a fucking dime. That money will be donated to charities and families of your victims. I'll withdraw all of it. You hear me, muthafucka!" Malcolm screamed, but the phone went dead.

"Tell me we got them." Malcolm anxiously stared at Sheldon who managed the trace program after Veronica had started it.

"We don't," Sheldon said flatly.

Malcolm threw his cell phone, and it shattered into pieces.

Everett motioned for his team to leave; he'd regroup with them shortly.

He followed Malcolm into his office.

"Hey, I know how hard it is to feel like you have no power. I've lost men and women before and it doesn't get easier along the way, but you are the best option we have in finding Avery. We are going to turn the pressure up on Crusher's associates until someone talks but we need..." Everett paused to make eye contact with Malcolm.

"Avery needs you. Whatever it takes but we gotta think realistically. If we give Crusher the cryptocurrency back, well that's just not an option. We need a location. I'm going to make a few phone calls and get some off the books help if we need it. Let's just hope it doesn't come down to what I think it will." Everett walked out of Malcolm's lab. He made eye contact with Sheldon who nodded in understanding; his boss didn't have his head completely in the game.

"Everett."

Veronica was calling out to him.

"We still may get a location on the call. The program boss man created is still working somehow."

Everett wasn't sure how that worked but trusted the information.

"As soon as you get something call me."

He turned and walked out the lab

The chief of police had called captain Montgomery into her office for an update on where the investigation stood. She had been getting pushback in some areas where Commissioner Grahl had allies and had been summoned by the mayor to ask if she knew about the financial ties being uncovered that the detectives had questioned him about.

"Keep at it. Everything you're doing has them in a panic. The escalations between Crusher and his rival was expected; wounded animals are often easy prey." The chief was adding her signature to paperwork of officers retiring from active duty.

"I received Jimmy's badge in the mail after..." Captain Montgomery watched the chief's eyes roll up from the papers to meet his.

"I've got officers that I trust providing protection for my immediate team's loved ones, but the team is beating down doors and shaking the hornet's nest." Captain left out that Avery had been abducted, and that was where the team's attention had gone.

"The Feds were up my ass investigating our police force the last three years. It takes more than their recommended suggestions to clean up what we both know has been out of whack for a long time. Twelve officers so far?" The chief asked in reference to how many officers bank accounts had received deposits from a Crusher entity.

"Yes, ma'am, twelve so far, but we have only gone through about forty percent of the information we have. When do you want us to move on either one of them?" The captain and chief knew they had overwhelming evidence against the commissioner and a strong case against the mayor.

A knock on the door from the chief's secretary interrupted their conversation.

"Excuse me, chief." She walked to turn on the television.

"I thought you would want to see this." She stared up at the screen.

The commissioner was giving a press conference at the entrance of City Hall in the rain. He was in full uniform with adornment. The overhang from the entrance blocked most of the rain from reaching the reporters and media outlets from getting wet. Those with cameras were trying to find the best camera angles and added protection for their equipment from the rain.

"Turn it up." Captain Montgomery stood up and walked across the carpet to stand in front of the television.

"Law enforcement officers are some of the bravest and most dedicated people I know. I've served the community for over forty years, and I can tell you the loss of Mario Laughlin hits a little differently. For those of you who knew him, he will be sorely missed. I never had children, but he was like a son to me." The commissioner paused as it appeared he got choked up. "Effective immediately, I will be taking a short time off. I'm sure that you, the media will find a way to spin this story and my words, and that's nothing new. I haven't taken a vacation in over five years so write that too." He stared at the reporters momentarily before the first question was fired at him.

"Sir, sir. There have been reports that Officer Mario Laughlin was murdered in retaliation for the investigations into Derrick Crusher, is there any truth to that?" A woman's voice was heard above the others.

"Mario Laughlin's death is being investigated and I can't commit on an ongoing investigation. Derrick Crusher is not the topic. This is about..."

"If the allegations are true, is it out of line to talk about any possible connection? Isn't this line of questioning pertinent?" The woman reporter quickly followed up.

The commissioner was becoming agitated.

"Listen, you are typically fair and what I can share with you at this time is that this is an ongoing investigation. Now if you have another question I can answer." He took charge of the moment. He had been in this role long enough to know how to pivot onto a different topic.

"Thank you, Commissioner, is it true, that recent revelations have come to light that may shine a new perspective in the shooting of your partner Officer Kuper over thirty years ago?" The follow up question silenced everyone.

The commissioner was frozen.

"Officer Kuper was a good man. Thank you for your time." The commissioner abruptly left the press conference, returning inside of city hall.

Captain Montgomery stared at the television. The chief was on the phone speaking with someone. She was livid that she had no forewarning.

"If the press pool is congregating, don't you think that means something! To my office right now!" She hung up the phone.

"I didn't know you were still running that

investigation." She looked across her desk at him.

"I had them stop looking into it, but Crusher has some damaging evidence on those he got to come and work for his side. Forensics ran across it and my team advised me of it. Nothing was pursued." The captain had not been ordered by the chief to back off the thirty-year old case, that was something he chose months ago to focus on the present.

"Have Malcolm and the lab find out the truth about Kuper when we have this situation under control. I expect a call from the mayor's office sometime soon.

"Unless there's something else we need to discuss?" She posed the question to Captain Montgomery.

He thought about updating her on the abduction, but with so many things on her plate, he felt confident that he could manage.

"No ma'am, I don't have anything else."

The chief stood up from her desk to walk David out.

"You're the one person I trust who I know has not been compromised. We are on the cusp of getting our city back, let's not blow it. Dismissed."

Captain Montgomery walked out of the office and bumped into the man and woman the chief had summoned when his phone rang.

The display was from Laura Kuper-Coates. Undoubtedly, she had seen the press conference and had more questions. He let it go to voicemail.

With real time decisions to be made, he would wait to check it later, there was too much to be done.

Gwen watched the press conference from her hotel suite. She was on the phone speaking with someone.

"The commissioner has done exactly what he was told. The press conference went better than expected. The reporter opened up an old wound, should we let him bleed out slowly?" She asked the person on the other line.

She listened intently to the directive she was being given.

"Understood."

The call ended.

Gwen showered and dressed. Her next appointment was with a state senator and city council member who were highly influential. The plan to replace the commissioner was under way, but each step had to be forged so his departure felt authentic.

She looked over the information she would use to pressure them if the briefcase of cash was insufficient. One of her cell phones rang.

"This is Gwen."

"Who the fuck told him to take a break when my ass is on the line. I need every asset working to make this go away. I said I would handle my business!" Crusher's voice came through the handset loudly.

"I've repaid the advance when my funds were low, I expect the same autonomy that I've always had and earned!" He finished.

Gwen took a deep breath before responding.

"Derrick, I am not your enemy. I'm not against you, but you will lower your voice when you and I speak. It's disrespectful to me and the relationship we have built over the course of our business. He got the order from me. It's what's needed now. You can do what needs to be done but, the commissioner is off limits. She placed her files in her black leather bag.

"What I need to be done is for him to have been doing his job." Crusher's tone was still aggressive, but the loudness had dwindled.

"Be that as it may, off limits. I understand you have a lead on your money. You're taking risks, big risks and I hope the payoff is worth it. I guess with the whole city barreling down on you, concentrating on 10% of your wealth is a smart play to you. Use the intelligence that got you to this point instead of letting your ego take charge again. I will speak with you later. I'm running late for a meeting." She hung up without him getting another word in.

Gwen took one more look around her hotel suite. She secured the .22 caliber gun under her pant leg and walked out the door.

Everett's team had hit the city, turning over every rock possible to get any information on Avery. He and Cole checked their usual CI's and even Turtle, but he didn't know anything about Avery's abduction.

Vania beat down her former department's door but all she got from them was Crusher was going to war with his rivals, and the four dead bodies found in the city of Bexley was a reminder to his competition that he still was in control. Travis spoke with Rafi and confirmed what Vice shared with Vania; war was on the doorstep of the capital city.

Everett was listening to a voicemail that Keiko had left when Captain Montgomery walked back into the office.

"The only thing that he understands is force or leverage. We are going to disrupt his business, all of it. I want the file pulled on his lieutenants and soldiers, if they have jay walking violations, I want them arrested. I want all the businesses he has sent money to touched. There will be a heavy presence of The Thin Blue line wherever he goes. Two and two from here on out, all the time." The captain made it clear that any investigations conducted required them to be done with partners. No one was to be left to fend for themselves."

"What does the lab have?" he asked no one directly but expected an answer.

"Sheldon is waiting for the composition of paint to yield results. Malcolm tapped into the city's camera feeds. He saw a vehicle speeding away from Avery's after the abduction and ran it down. A couple had been fighting and one of them drove away in a rush." Everett put his phone down.

"So, nothing..." Captain Montgomery hesitated and looked at the team.

"What are you waiting for, go turn his life upside down. The commissioner can't run interference right now." He left them and walked into his office, closing the door behind.

"It's about damn time the gloves come off." Cole twisted his neck.

"Two uniforms to walk the block of his restaurant twenty-four seven. We will put a tail on Crusher and just let him know we are there like mosquitoes. Travis and V.A. find out about the restaurant manager and see who the other guy was speaking German. I want an update every two hours." Everett slid his chair back, walked to Captain Montgomery's door, and knocked. He went in and closed it behind him.

Travis was already on the computer looking up the name of the manager from the new restaurant on the website.

'Aaron Wiertel.' He read the bio and then started background on him using all the tools at his fingertips.

Cole walked into the break-room to return with two mugs of coffee.

"V.A. next time don't only get dark roasted." He mustered a small grin.

"There won't be a next..." she went to respond, but Everett called Cole away. They took the stairwell exit.

"Aaron Wiertel has been managing high-end restaurants for over twenty years. He is kinda the who's who for the industry. The man speaking with him was his brother Max." Travis turned his computer so his partner could see.

"They both have squeaky clean records since

immigrating to America as teens over forty years ago, but..." Travis paused to turn his computer back to face him, pulling up their family history and government documents. He turned the computer back toward Vania, who looked at the screen.

"Konig-Wiertel?"

"Yeah Konig." Travis stood up to take his computer to the captain.

"T, what are you doing?" Vania scooted her chair out to block him.

"We have a legitimate reason to ask to speak with the Senator to see why he allows his family to be in bed with Crusher." Travis was eager.

"Where's the connection besides surnames?" Vania asked.

"Ivan Konig-Wiertel is the older brother of Katlyn Konig-Wiertel. The mother of Senator Konig and we know she still has strong ties to Germany." Travis answered like she should have known this information.

"How the hell do you know this?"

"I do background on people I vote for..." He paused and picked up his cell. He texted Everett the information and asked if he should pass it on. Everett said he would take care of it and for the young partners to assist Malcolm in tracking down who carried the paint in question.

"That's great T. I didn't say we shouldn't investigate but we just didn't have to tell him yet."

Travis shook his head. He wasn't in the mood to be second guessed again.

"We have to help Malcolm." He stood up and left her sitting. He took the stairwell to the lab and was talking to Malcolm when she walked in.

"So, I've got a list of contractors who ordered this specific paint. There are only five that make the list. I will take two and you take these three." Malcolm handed them the information.

"Yeah, no. That doesn't work for us. We all can go together, there's safety in numbers and to be honest, it's you that Crusher wants. So, we all should..." Vania was attempting to reason.

"Do what I just asked you. I do outrank both of you and I can take care of myself, remember you all were chasing my marks at the academy." He pulled his white lab coat back to revel a 9mm holstered in his belt.

"I can handle it." Malcolm ushered them out of his lab. With any luck, Avery would be found before the days end.

"I thought we were headed to pick up Spade and squeeze him." Cole watched Everett drive in the exact opposite direction programmed in the GPS.

"The manager from the restaurant is actually a Konig. One child lost the surname, and another kept it." Everett knew the area he was driving but had Cole upload into the system.

"Senator Konig, and his family have major influence and a small empire overseas." Cole added.

Everett knew the history of the family. He had done special ops work in Germany. The intel wasn't complete at the time, but the rumor was they were tied to very old money.

"If Aaron and Max are truly Konig's, under the guise of Wiertel; then they have a say in what's going on now surrounding Crusher. Our goal right now is to get Avery back alive and take Crusher out of the picture."

Cole listened carefully to his partner's choice of words. Everett had not said apprehend or arrest. "Take Crusher out the picture" felt ominous. Cole was okay with whatever happened, as long as their target was hit.

They pulled up to a gated community. The homes behind the gates made Cole think back to some of the multi-million-dollar mansions that frequented Los Angeles, California. Several styles of homes were spaced out and as they looked inward, the winding road added to the view.

"Detectives Kennedy and Clark with the Columbus Police Department. We're here to see Aaron or Max Wiertel."

"Do you have an appointment?"

Everett glanced at Cole, who shook his head in bewilderment.

"No, no appointment but we need to speak with them." Everett was polite but firm.

There was a delay in the security guard's response and when he replied Everett was at a loss of words.

"I'm sorry, but they aren't receiving any guests at this time. Thank you."

Cole started to yell but Everett beat him to it.

"We are detectives with the..." but he was caught off.

"Detective, the Wiertels are not seeing guests today, please leave, as this is private property, without a warrant you will take your leave."

"What's your name?" Everett was going to threaten him if need be to get access inside of the gate.

"My name is none of your business, but as a courtesy,

my former badge number is 1530. Come back when you have an appointment or a warrant."

"They have the best tortilla soup in this city, don't you think? The commissioner turned me on to this about five years ago. A mom-and-pop restaurant is where true business comes from. You have to start off with just an idea." Gwen was sitting down at one of eight outdoor picnic benches. The smell of spices moved across the neighborhood with the shifting of the wind.

Crusher wasn't pleased to have had to make a detour to take this impromptu meeting. He had spent the last three hours of his afternoon taking his police 'escort' on a wild goose chase, only to lose them after switching vehicles being used as decoys.

"I have business to attend to." Crusher noticed the black SUV sitting in the parking lot. It made him feel uneasy. He nodded at Spade to check it out, but Gwen stopped him.

"They're here on Institution business..." Gwen paused and looked in the direction of the SUV.

"You've always been an asset, and I'm rooting for you Derrick, but you have to get your business in order soon."

A server brought out two bags of food for Gwen.

"Empanadas?" She offered Derrick the pastry delight.

"No...." He paused as she stood up.

"If you're done summoning me, I can get back to getting my money and pressing my 'assets' around the city." Derrick held his tone in check.

"By all means, I have to clean up some of your spillover." She walked away toward the SUV. The driver's side window lowered and a man both Crusher and Spade recognized waved at them.

Gwen looked back over the hood of the SUV at Crusher before getting in. He rolled the window back up and they pulled off.

"Did you know he was in town?" Crusher asked as they made their way back to their vehicle.

Crusher knew things were escalating, and he needed to get his house back in order.

One of the two soldiers accompanying Crusher closed the back door after Crusher got in.

"Hell, no. I had no idea. Max said nothing." Spade had already pulled his cell phone out and was texting one of the Wiertel brothers.

"No let that ride for now. We still have the thief at the warehouse?" Crusher was assured Avery was still secured.

Crusher needed him alive.

"Have Benji bring a computer. We haven't broken his hands or fingers, have we?" Crusher was going to add incentive for Avery.

"No, some ribs and he's lost a few teeth. Nothing major," one of the soldiers answered.

"Stop at Lowe's. We need to turn up the heat."

"All these damn buildings look the same." Vania started complaining as they walked into the third warehouse on the list Malcolm gave them. A huge open space with large shelves housing industrial products. A woman approached them on a golf cart in a security officer's uniform.

Vania pulled out her badge before the woman tried to posture for positioning.

"Officers, how can I help you?" She asked.

"Our records show that this is one of the locations this paint was shipped to, can you tell us if you have this in stock or the last time you did?" Travis showed her the paperwork.

"Darlene has to look this up. I just drive around and make people nervous. Hop on."

Travis watched Vania take the seat up front, leaving him to sit on the back of the cart.

The business offices were on the opposite side of the building. The young detectives had entered through the employee entrance.

"Darlene, these are police officers can you help them with inventory?"

A tiny woman standing barely 5'0 was standing outside her office looking at the workers.

"They got a warrant?" Her voice was strong and caught both detectives off guard.

"No, no warrant but honestly there's no proprietary risk or infringement of anyone's rights..."

Travis spoke quickly to prevent a possible pissing match with Darlene and his partner.

Darlene laughed and waved them into her office.

"Just busting your chops. Let me see that."

Travis handed her the paper.

She pressed some buttons in her keyboard and checked inventory numbers.

"Yeah, we've got some in stock, and we haven't..." She checked something else in her computer.

"Sold it to anyone this quarter. It's pretty high-end paint."

"Can you tell us what companies, within the state ordered it?" Travis had a hunch and was hoping he was right.

"Yeah, I can, that's in another system though. I won't ask what this is about. I stand behind the boys in blue and women in blue." Darlene paused.

"The only contractor using this was that company for the downtown project, the restaurant club office space. DC Construction," she finished.

Vania's eyebrows raised.

"Do you mind printing that off? Thank you so much." Vania showed her appreciation.

Travis thanked her again.

Travis was calling Everett to update them when they walked out. The sun had gone down and they realized they were at the opposite end of where they entered.

Vania listened to Travis speaking on the phone and thought it just as important to let Malcolm know they had found a lead. She called and it went straight to voicemail.

"Yeah we saw him about three hours ago. We did

everything to work together but he gave us an order. Being honest I have no idea what his rank is." Travis was explaining when he was interrupted by Vania.

"I just called him and straight to voicemail."

Everett's voice came through after hearing Vania, so Travis put the call on speaker.

"Everyone has been trying to get a hold of him. Meet us at the lab, we can regroup there." The phone call ended.

"Shit, we should've just gone with him." Travis was rationalizing the decision to leave Malcolm alone.

"No, we shouldn't have. Malcolm and Everett have the same rank. He just doesn't broadcast it." Vania looked up as they rounded the corner of the parking lot.

"I guess, he should be alright. He was packing some heat." Travis shook his head as he thought back to Malcolm being strapped.

"With his scores still untouched at the academy, I'm sure he can use it too."

They finally reached their vehicle and got in.

Vania tried calling Malcolm again, but it went to the messaging system again immediately.

"He's okay, right, T?"

Malcolm thought it was odd that the same two men passed each other three times as they walked the perimeter of the second location he was checking. Another man exited the building to replace what Malcolm determined were sentries. He waited a few minutes to time his approach not to be seen. He had the cover of darkness on his side. He wanted to case what he could without being seen.

He kept to the shadows as he approached and entered the building where the sentry had exited. He moved along the shelves holding material. Boxes were stacked intermittently between what appeared to be construction equipment. Two small excavators sat opposite each other and a few flatbed trucks.

Stairs ran up the sides of the building to two top levels.

Malcolm heard voices and knelt. He moved a few rows over and slid a box to the side to give him a better view.

Four men were sitting down at a table playing dominoes and drinking alcohol. His eyes shifted as a fifth man walking across the floor drew his attention.

Malcolm saw another group of roughly five men and a woman sitting around. One from the group got up with a bottled water and walked out of his line of sight.

Malcolm crept along the aisle to remain hidden.

That's when he saw Avery tied to a chair, beaten and bloodied.

His first instinct was to engage but he knew that was the wrong course of action. He backed out slowly, retracing his steps to get out clean.

Two more people walked one of the side aisles adjacent to his position, so he had to lay flat against the floor. Once they passed, he moved with more urgency back to the door he entered.

Malcolm checked each side to make sure the sentries weren't seen. He opened the door and snuck out. He moved with haste back to his vehicle. He had to wait for two vehicles to pass before crossing the street.

In that moment everything slowed down as the second vehicle slammed on its brakes.

Malcolm stood motionless as the back window rolled down and he was face to face with Derrick Crusher.

The intensity in Derrick's eyes matched his voice.

"Malcolm, we were just looking for you."

"That's good work b-team. With this we should be able to get a warrant for his businesses. Malcolm still hasn't checked back in." Cole was getting worried, as was the rest of the team.

Everett was speaking with Captain Montgomery about getting a rush on the warrants they needed.

"Voicemail again." Vania tried Malcolm.

Veronica and Yari walked from a back office, and from their facial expressions, something was terribly wrong.

"We can't find his phone." Veronica shared that they had tried to run a trace, but no signal existed within range of the cell towers they had access to.

Everyone looked at Everett to determine what to do next.

"Gear up, until we find Malcolm we don't rest. You two didn't get a full list of sites, and he cleared his web history. Veronica there's no way to pull up what he searched?" Everett asked

"It will take time, I already have a program sorting what it can, but it will take time." She shook her head, as Yari places her hand in her shoulder for reassurance.

"We have help that arrived an hour ago. We've been playing by the same old rule book with our hands tied. Tonight, we take the gloves off and if anyone doesn't feel they should be a part of this – tell me now."

Everett made eye contact with everyone, and each person was all in.

Sheldon came flying out of Malcolm's office with a laptop computer.

"Okay, I've got him, or the last location the signal came through." Sheldon faces the screen towards the others.

"His technology, well Avery's technology; Malcolm has it in his belt and shoes." He said flatly.

"Shelly, you are the fucking man!!!" Cole kissed him on the cheek.

"Meet me in one hour. Like I said gear up. Tonight, we play for keeps." Everett walked out leaving his team behind.

"We have the element of surprise for once on our side. Let's keep it that way. Get your gear and get ready." Cole issued secondary orders

"I'm coming." Yari said.

"You don't have time to get clearance and you can't afford this risk we're taking." Travis interjected.

Yari went to reply but Veronica interceded.

"He's right."

Yari looked at her with a puzzled look.

"We can get tech support ready. We need to charge drones and other surveillance; you can help me with that?" Veronica pulled Yari away while Everett and the young detectives followed him out.

"They don't need distractions tonight. We can support from a distance but if it all goes wrong..." Veronica didn't say another word.

They both knew what the team was doing tonight for Malcolm skirted the law.

"Veronica and Agent Yari, I need your assistance in the field. We will run tech, this is our team and if one of us goes down, we all go down. Do you concur?"

Veronica looked at Yari.

"We concur."

"I can't remember the last time I had chicken tortilla soup from them. Thank you, Gwen." The commissioner sat at his dining room table opening the bag of food she had brought for him. He looked vastly different in an OSU T-shirt and blue jeans. His potbelly protruded out, and only his suspenders kept his pants from falling.

"It's been a long career for you, and we know retiring

early wasn't the plan, but this little extra incentive should make up for any loss of benefits you may incur." She smiled and nodded at the gym bag of cash lying next to his feet.

"It will be more than enough, and Crusher will understand my departure? The last time we had a misunderstanding my assistant ended up dead. He was a cop you know?" The commissioner sighed to indicate it was the cost of being in business with a crime syndicate. He understood the risk, but nothing had ever hit so closely to home.

"It's what has to be done, his understanding is not required. I want you to know that the relationship we developed over the years was critical and we thank you." She opened her bag of food and asked for a spoon.

"I just can't do plastic utensils. I wasn't sure if you like empanadas, but I brought a few extra." She dove into her soup and he did the same.

"Maybe in my retirement I'll invest in my own restaurant or invest in them because this food, although bad for my health, is comforting right now." He coughed attempting to clear his throat.

Gwen set back in her chair, pulled out her phone, and made a call.

"Yes, it's done." She smiled at him as he scooped another portion of soup into his spoon.

"It's spicier than I remember, but good." He said lowly as she ended the call.

He rubbed his neck feeling the increase in heat from the soup. He drank half the glass of water in front of him before tugging on his shirt.

"Are you ok?" Gwen watched as his spoon slowly dropped from his hand to splash soup back onto him.

He couldn't breathe.

A man emerged from the front room of his home wearing all black with gloves.

"Of course, you're not ok. I want you to know that everything I said about our relationship with you being critical over the years is true." She stood up and slipped on gloves.

The commissioner's throat had closed, and he was having a reaction to the food. He tried sucking in air but only trace amounts made its' way to his lungs.

The man in black began cleaning up the food and wiping down the areas Gwen had touched.

"It's also true commissioner that you had one simple charge to keep Crusher protected. You failed at that...." She paused to take one final look at him turn blue.

"But because you were a decent associate, shellfish has been mixed in with your soup."

The commissioner tried standing and fell face forward.

Gwen waited to confirm he was dead before she and her associate in black made one final pass and then departed.

Everett provided the location for the team to meet when they arrived, they didn't expect to see four men dressed in combat gear.

"We are all family here and our goal is to retrieve family and finally dismantle everything Crusher has touched. The building layouts are up to date. It's almost twenty thousand square feet. Standard warehouse. Sheldon will fly a drone in undetected to get us eyes on. Once we are set, two separate teams will move up the stairs on each side of the building until they reach adequate vantage points.

Travis and I will advance directly forward with V.A. and Cole protecting our backside. We need to expect the worst. We have two friendlies and everyone else is a combatant." Everett had already shown his military brother's photos of both Malcolm and Avery.

"Everybody, Sheldon has our coms linked. We don't come back unless everyone comes back. Any questions?"

No one asked anything. Everyone present knew the gravity of the actions they were taking.

"One last thing and this is an order. Shoot to kill."

"Hoo Rah!" Black yelled out followed by his compatriots.

They grabbed their gear and walked out, leaving Everett to have one last word.

"I don't have anything else, do any of you have questions?"

"We don't." Cole spoke up for everyone.

"Sheldon, keep your distance with the surveillance van. Veronica you are his second eyes and Yari since you insist on coming, keep them protected." Everett walked out of the room with his team in tow.

Captain Montgomery finished looking over the last bit of evidence he needed to bring the commissioner in for questioning. He had the older detective Jack and his partner Bryan drive him for backup. When they arrived, the garage lights activated sensing movement from their car.

A neighbor's dog had gotten loose with them yelling behind.

"Lita, get back her...come here honey!" The dog returned to its' owner and ran into the garage before it closed behind.

"Well, he's still up, front light is on," Jack said. He wasn't sure that this was the right move to make or better yet the timing of it, but he backed his captain's leadership.

The captain rang the doorbell and stood squarely in front of the door. He had waited over thirty years to be able to question him and now with proof, solid evidence he would get to the truth of everything, including Officer Kuper.

He rang the buzzer again in succession.

"His cars in the garage." Bryan had returned from the side of the garage where two small windows were situated.

"Stay here and cover the front, Jack come with me." Captain Montgomery walked across the front lawn and shrubs and the long side of the home. There were no signs of foul play. He unlatched the back wooden fence and walked on a small stone path to reach the back patio. He knocked on the rear patio glass and Jack pulled a deck chair to stand on. He investigated through the kitchen window overlooking the back yard.

"Captain, I see a body. It's Commissioner Grahl laying on the floor!" Jack tried the window and it opened. Captain Montgomery yelled for Bryan. He was small enough to fit through the window to unlock the doors for entry.

Jack had already called for an ambulance before the commissioner's vitals were taken.

"He's dead." Captain Montgomery shook his head in disbelief.

Bryan walked back to the vehicle for gloves and foot coverings to keep the space from being contaminated. They checked the home for any signs of forced entry or foul play. Nothing seemed amiss.

"Did the pressure get to him, captain?" Bryan watched his leader sitting at the table staring at the dead body.

"Maybe detective, maybe."

Sheldon parked the surveillance van two blocks away and had launched the miniature drone. Small in capacity, it made up for it with technology and stealth. Veronica observed the monitors and Yari kept an ear on the team on the com system from the van.

"Ok, I'm inside. The connection is good." Sheldon hovered the drone inside the warehouse and moved it slowly in the space.

"There's five people on the second level northwest section." Yari relayed through the coms.

Everett motioned for two members from the military to move as planned up the right stairs and the other two to take the left. He had learned from countless missions in the military that position was key, so they moved to secure those vantage points.

"There are heavily armed guards, I see submachine guns and they're moving on the first level away from your location...at least another eight."

Yari kept relaying where the perpetrators were stationed and then she went silent and Veronica gasped.

"Agent." Everett's voice came through for intel.

"Sorry, Malcolm and Avery have been located. First floor, about forty meters from your position...you won't miss them. It's bad." Yari watched as each group of two took the stairs. They carried P90's and MP7 as their primary weapons, with several more for backup.

Everett knew he had the best men he could wish for covering him and as he watched them move, he and Travis took down the center of the warehouse with heightened senses.

CHAPTER SIX: A BEGINNING

"Two bogeys on your six." Yari relayed what she saw from the drone.

Veronica's eyes lit up when the drone was seen, and shots were fired at it.

In an instant, the silence was replaced with chaos.

The elite forces had pushed through those on the second floor and were now shooting down at roughly two dozen armed men.

"Get those muthafuckas! Y'all came to the wrong place today!" Spade's voice called out as his group returned fire.

"On your six, your six god-dammit!" Yari's voice yelled into their coms repeatedly.

Cole saw the shadow before he saw the body and let two rounds off. One bad guy dropped.

The sound of the discharge created attention to be drawn to their approach.

The elite group still rained bullets down and had made many of the criminals take shelter, but it drove the larger group into the other team's space.

Everett had his Mossberg 590A1 firmly against his shoulder and looking down his sights. He pulled the trigger, and a body dropped. He pulled again, and another body dropped.

Vania moved with precision of the training they all had

undergone. She checked her blind spots before advancing to cover Everett's flank.

"Travis at your three!" Yari's voice came through, and he reacted and put two bullets into a suspect's chest center mass.

Bullet casings flew everywhere and those who were not fatally shot, were crawling for cover.

"Reload!" Everett called out after being shot at and using his last of seven rounds in his shotgun.

Travis moved forward and laid down shots as Everett reloaded.

Everett nodded at Travis, and they began moving forward again.

Vania saw Cole in pursuit of two suspects as he moved up to a position on the second level. He shot one who fell to the first floor. Vania covered him but didn't see a culprit rounding the corner until the last minute. She fired two rounds and then lowered her position. When the gunman stuck his head out to look, she got a shot off into his shoulder. He staggered from his position and fell into Vania who spent her last bullets from her magazine into him.

Another perpetrator emerged and took aim and fired. She shielded herself with the body of the man she had just shot. The weight prevented her from exchanging magazines, and as she heard the last cartridge expended, she looked up to see the man charging her with his fists raised.

Vania allowed the dead body to drop to the floor as the first punch was swung. She dodged it by contorting her body to one side and slipped his second punch. Her momentum gave her an enormous amount of torque when she punched him on the inside of his knee at the weakest point.

"AAGH!" he screamed out as his knee gave way.

Vania used her return momentum to strike him squarely in the jaw as he crumbled. With her last blow, she struck him in the back of the neck with her elbow. She moved quickly to retrieve her weapon, and that's when she saw the gun extended, pointing at her.

A blur came from nowhere and pushed her out the way before she got shot. The perp fired and struck Cole in the back shoulder; he was quick enough to return fire as soon as he hit the ground.

Vania changed magazines and then pulled Cole to safety, and they realized he was bleeding.

"That's going to leave a mark."

The gunfire lessened, and Yari saw the garage door open as Crusher and a few men tried to flee. They grabbed Malcolm, but Everett pulled his handgun and aimed before

Malcolm could be dragged out.

Crusher saw Everett switch from his shotgun to handgun. He pulled one of his soldiers in front of him to take the bullets.

Travis took aim and shot a guard who tried sneaking up on Everett. The bullet zipped by Everett and landed squarely in the suspects head.

Everett kept firing at Crusher as he escaped with three men. The firing settled.

Everett told his elite friends to leave before the police showed up, and they would meet them at his home when everything calmed down. Each man knew the acts they had taken were illegal and against military code. The things they had sacrificed for each other in war had helped create their own code, which outweighed all others. They would do anything for one another.

The first ambulance on the scene took Cole and Avery. Cole didn't seem to be phased by being shot, but Everett knew he was in shock.

"I've seen worse," he joked with Cole when he was being wheeled out.

"Avery is barely alive and may not make it. His ribs are broken, and he may be hemorrhaging he's being rushed to OSU Medical. Malcolm's jaw is broken, and his shoulder separated." Sheldon updated Everett who was walking to see Malcolm.

His face was bruised badly, amongst his other injuries. He sat on the edge of a gurney and watched Everett approach. He motioned him forward with his good arm. He waved him even closer and pushed out five words through the pain.

"It took you long enough."

Everett nodded as the two young detectives joined him.

"What about Crusher?" Travis asked. He and Vania had already checked on Malcolm and were returning from speaking with Veronica and Yari who were still in the van erasing the footage of the assault.

"He's done. We've issued an immediate warrant for his arrest. There is a tri-state bolo... We've done our job," Everett finished as Travis pointed to Malcolm.

"Boss, let us get you checked up," An EMT urged Malcolm.

Malcolm stood up slowly and winced and looked at the remaining team.

"Thank you." Malcolm walked away before any of them could see him crying.

Spade drove like a bat out of hell back to the loft. He knew that the window for escape was closing.

"Who were those muthafuckas? I saw the locals, but who the fuck was with 'em?" Crusher kept yelling and ignoring Gwen's phone calls.

"When we get in here, I'm grabbing cash, and we have to go. They will be on our tail, and if we don't get out now, we never will," he finished.

"Sir, it might be a good idea to get Gwen involved. Get some cover and some time for a good plan." Spade was being diplomatic and smart. He believed Crusher still had value to Gwen's employers. Fleeing would only exacerbate everything.

"Fuck Gwen, fuck, fuck, fuck Gwen. If that bitch would've got out of my way, most of this shit would've been resolved now. The commissioner and mayor still work for me!" Crusher bellowed out. The ensuing silence was awkward.

"Sir, the commissioner is dead," one of the other men in the car relayed the news.

Crusher pounded on the front seat; he couldn't control his emotions.

They pulled into the remote entry to his loft, moved

quickly inside, and up the elevator. He told the two men with him to wait downstairs and no one was to enter. He took Spade with him to his personal space.

"I don't care who it is. If they get off that elevator, kill em."

Crusher ran into his back rooms and pulled bags out, already filled with money. He reached into his closet for a portable safe and removed his passport and travel documents. He looked around the room to see if he was leaving anything valuable. He moved from his bedroom into his office as fast as he could. This would be the last time he set foot in this city.

Spade guarded the elevator. He glanced out onto the balcony and saw the skyline of the city. Of all the cities he had been to, Columbus was one of the better ones. Now he was on the run with his boss and the feeling of uncertainty created tension in his chest.

Spade saw the elevator light blink, and it was on the move up to the loft. He pulled his gun out and stepped to the side, so he had a quicker line of sight than whoever exited.

The elevator went past the club and office exit. It came to rest on the Loft level.

Spade readied himself and took aim. When the doors opened, he made eye contact before he pulled the trigger.

He didn't add the required amount of pressure to discharge the weapon. He holstered his weapon and got on the elevator and pressed down.

Crusher came back out with two large duffel bags full of money and was ignoring another call from Gwen.

"We have to go right...." The words stuck in his throat when he saw the man in black sitting at the long meeting table. His eyes relayed that fear was not an adequate emotion.

"Hey, I was just about to..." Crusher fell to the ground with a gunshot to his head.

The man in black verified the kill and then took the elevator back down.

Spade was waiting on him; the two men who had been stationed were no longer there.

"You've been loyal to The Institution. We will take care of any police matters that may come about. Everything that he has in the loft is yours." Spade watched him walk out the door into a waiting car.

The team rushed to Crush Groove with members of the task force assigned to them. The restaurant was closed along with the club associated with it. Max Wiertel threatened to sue the police force for unlawful entry, but with Crusher being identified in connection with the kidnapping and torture of law enforcement, exigent circumstances overruled the right to a warrant.

Everett ordered Max's brother to give them access to Crusher's private elevator, and he declined because he did not have access. The task force was set up to override the elevator gaining access to Everett and his team. They readied themselves, not knowing what to expect when the doors opened.

Cole and Travis panned right while Everett and Vania took the opposite side.

Money was scattered across the floor, and there was an eerie silence before Crusher's body was noticed with a gunshot to the head.

After securing the loft area, Cole had the coroner's office enter.

"Someone got to him first." Everett related to Captain Montgomery over the phone while Cole and the b-team watched Crusher being rolled away in a blackbody bag.

Travis laughed uncontrollably and it becomes infectious.

"So ends the reign of Derrick Crusher." Vania and Travis smiled at each other and nodded.

Cole looked at her and then at Travis realizing they had not completed the thought process.

"And a beginning of someone else's...."

The private airport was nearly empty except for the two guards who allowed access to the private area. The white Mercedes Benz pulled to the security gate and waited until they opened the electric fence. The Cessna Citation X had been prepared for flight and cleared for takeoff.

The man in black emerged from the front passenger door. He opened the rear door to allow Gwen out of the car. The driver, Aaron Wiertel, removed two suitcases from the trunk and rolled them to the bottom of the airplane stairs.

"When should we expect new directives?" Aaron asked the man in black.

The assassin glanced back at Gwen to indicate if there was an answer to his question, then Gwen had it.

Gwen stood by the Mercedes and sent a text to Spade.

"You have been a loyal employee. Think about if you'd like anything else besides the duffel bags you received as compensation for your service. We will be in touch."

...THREE MONTHS LATER

"I know it's been a long time coming, and so many ups and downs. It's been worth it and thank you, David. My family and my father thank you." Laura Kuper-Coates was nearly in tears as she listened to the facts as he had found them to be. Her father was an honorable man, and his partner at the time was not. Tied into criminals he got a kick back for looking the other way. The suspect who had gotten away with shooting his partner was tied into some politicians. The former commissioner was paid off to lie and was backed by those same politicians.

"It was my team. I had given up, not because I wanted to, but because everything else. I'm sorry if that is offensive, but its honest."

Johanna listened to her husband on the phone and her daughter explaining that she wasn't sure anymore, about getting married.

"DJ can't hear nothing about that right now, honey. In fact, Grandma needs to tell you something and I need you to listen, because I love you."

The daughter looked at her grandma who waved her forward. She placed both hands on the side of her granddaughter's face tenderly.

"You have to grow the fuck up, sweetie."

3 months

"I like when you teach us, auntie. Unc is okay, but you can take him." The nephews laughed together as they walked onto the mat at the Jiu Jitsu studio.

Vania had made it a point to keep something she enjoyed doing as a priority in her life.

Travis' nephews were quick learners and more humbled here than they were in their neighborhood. She understood out there they had to survive first, but inside these studio walls, they only had to strive to be better than they were yesterday.

"When this is over, are we still going to Becca's birthday party?" they asked.

"Lead the class, and the answer is yes."

The class was high intensity and she kept her word. She dropped them off at home to shower and change and did the same at her place.

She picked them back up and went to Robbi's home. They took Becca presents and were sitting down eating hamburgers and hot dogs in the back yard when Everett and Keiko arrived.

"Daddy!" Becca hollered and raced her brother to get a hug first.

"Hi, Ms. Keiko." Becca gave her a half-hug and accepted her birthday present.

"Hey, you two." Robbi was carrying more balloons and bubble making toys out.

"Hey, Robbi. The party is still going hard. What can I do to help?" Keiko asked.

"Sam is getting the ice cream and cake together, do

you mind?"

Keiko walked into the house with Mason leading the way,

"Somehow, we hold it all together, right?" Robbi handed Everett the balloons and walked back to the party.

"Indeed, we do Robbi. Indeed, we do."

3 months

Travis listened to Sirius XM as he drove. The jazz station was enough to clear his mind. He had thought about everything that transpired over the past year. The growth he had made as a detective and a person. He had made some mistakes along the way and had finally lessened up with his paperwork.

He thought about not taking the shot the first time they served Crusher a warrant or if he would've done anything differently with the uniformed officers who violated his mother's home. Two of them had lost their position with CPD, and the others were suspended in exchange for a lawsuit not being filed. Some officers who had learned what happened started a Go Fund Me page to help replace his mother's belongings. In the end, close to twenty thousand dollars was raised.

The gravest mistake he had made he was hoping to remedy.

He parked his car on the street and double checked the address. He was learning to be fearless.

He walked the driveway to the walkway leading to the front door. He hesitated to ring the buzzer, and before he pressed it, the door opened. He smiled and walked in and kissed Yari who closed the door behind him.

3 months

Malcolm pushed Avery around the car dealership. Recovery for them was a little longer as they also had to deal with the psychological toll of being tortured.

Avery had proven his loyalty to the team. He had been willing to sacrifice himself for people he had never spent time with.

Malcolm found that trait endearing and had been by his side ever since, prepping a room for him in his home. Now that Avery was feeling better, Malcolm wanted to surprise him by helping him get a brand-new car. It was a first step to appreciating life and wiping something off Avery's bucket list. He always wanted a new car, a convertible 5.0 Mustang.

Malcolm showed Avery how to negotiate to get the best deal when they walked into financing.

"So, how would you guys like to pay for this?" The finance manager was feeding paperwork through the printer for them to sign.

"He's going to use a line of credit or certified check," Malcolm advised.

The finance manager tried to get them to finance but Malcolm declined.

"I don't have..." Avery attempted to say but Malcolm handed him an envelope with banking information in his name.

Avery didn't understand, but Malcolm did. Derrick Crusher owed them both.

"You earned this."

Cole was feeling pain from being shot roughly ninety days ago. He had been on medical leave, and during that time, he had grown addicted to pain pills, and the once lively and outgoing man was now a shadow of the person he used to be. Rachel checked on him once a week, but he stopped taking calls from anyone outside of his team.

His beard had grown, and he wasn't keen on cutting it. He sent Becca a birthday card with two hundred dollars in it.

Veronica had consistently visited him and made sure he had food and didn't wallow in self-pity.

The knock on his door startled him because he was not expecting anyone. He ignored it until the doorbell was rung repeatedly.

"Okay, stop ringing my doorbell and bangin on my shit!" he yelled and opened the door.

He took a second look because an adolescent girl was staring at him with a book bag across her shoulders. Her sandy blonde hair was curly and her skin tanned.

"I'm not buying candy bars this year or ever again." He closed the door and walked away.

The girl banged on his door again.

"Detective Cole Kennedy?" she asked lowly.

"Listen, I don't want to buy anything that you're selling." He paused as she handed him a folder with documents.

"What's this?" Cole began to skim over the pages, and then he read them intently.

She walked into his house and sat down on his couch while he remained at the door with the papers in his hands.

"What? Wait , what the hell…" his voice trailed off as he looked at a picture from the woman that dumped him in college over fourteen years ago.

"I'm CJ, your daughter."

ABOUT THE AUTHOR

A.V. Smith is an athlete turned writer. With a passion for storytelling, he paints with words that captivate readers. Smith writes on an emotional level to empower readers to engage in deeper conversations about their past, their relationships, and their connection with the Universe. With his first book, "Madison: God's Fingerprint 1.618," he won the 2019 Author Academy Award for Best Romance. In "OHIO 10", Smith takes a break from romance and focuses his literary talent on crime and social issues that divide us.

Through life and love, Andre' has learned our steps are temporary, yet the journey intensely meaningful. This understanding led him to donate a kidney to his younger brother. As the father of three children, his desire is to see his children overcome the fear of success by being the best version of themselves. He strives to lead by example, at times falling short, but understanding human beings are still a work in progress. When he is not engaged in his passion, you can find him with a fishing pole in his hand, coaching youth level football, or attending a local artist event.

Other Books by A.V. Smith

While in college, Madison befriends a second-generation Colombian who gets bullied until she steps in. Madison receives more than a simple warm welcome when her friend takes her to visit Colombia for his family's gratitude. Unbeknownst to Madison, a familial bond is illuminated that changes her future. Love dares to awaken Madison's soul; however, with the darkness that surrounded her teenage years, she has constructed walls of protection.

As passionate, erotic themes and emotional conflict shift her vision of the world, she is forced to face the event that paralyzed her father and sent her parents to prison. The murder of a family of three combined with a harassing phone call at work puts Madison on a collision course with the man who had her friend's father assassinated, and who tainted the narcotics found in her father's possession the night her life was forever changed. Madison is a woman with a tumultuous past struggling to escape her demons all the while blindsided by love at a poetry event. Longing to feel normal, Madison attempts to balance her desire for justice with her need for swift, deadly punishment. With the help of her grandmother and sister-friends, she discovers who she really is as well as the courage to let love in.